Rollie and the Missing Six

Mystery Novels by Al Lamanda
City of Darkness

Rollie Finch Mysteries
One Upon a Time on 9/11
Rollie and the Missing Six

John Bekker Mysteries
Sunset
(Edgar Award Nominee for Best Novel)

Sunrise
(Voted Best Crime Novel of 2013 by the Maine Writers and Publishers Alliance)

First Light
(Nero Award Nominee)

This Side of Midnight
(Nero Award Nominee)

With Six You Get Wally
(Winner of the 2017 Nero Award for Best Mystery, and a Shamus Award Nominee)

Who Killed Joe Italiano
For Better or Worse
The Case of the Missing Fan Dancer

Western Novels as Ethan J. Wolfe
The Last Ride
The Regulator
The Range War of '82
Murphy's Law
All the Queen's Men
One If by Land

Rollie and the Missing Six

— A ROLLIE FINCH MYSTERY —

AL LAMANDA

Encircle Publications
Farmington, Maine, U.S.A.

Editor: Cynthia Brackett-Vincent
Cover design: Christopher Wait
Cover photograph © Getty Images

Published by:

Encircle Publications
PO Box 187
Farmington, ME 04938

Visit: http://encirclepub.com
info@ encirclepub.com

For the brave men and women of the United States Military.

CHAPTER ONE

Seated in a chair at the patio table in the backyard of his home in Queens, Rollie Finch watched his three daughters play with the family dog, Buddy, a six-month-old beagle. Recently neutered, the spot where he'd been shaved by the vet was still evident.

Since school was in session, Rollie took Buddy for his afternoon walks, and then the pup napped beside Rollie's desk in the office until the girls got home from school.

"Girls, it's getting late," Rollie said. "Time to start thinking about dinner."

"Okay, Dad," Grace said. Having just turned eighteen, Grace was the oldest of the three and a senior in high school.

Giselle was the middle daughter, having recently turned sixteen. The youngest was Gloria, who was fourteen and in the eighth grade.

Rollie went to his office. Twenty years ago, when Rollie and his wife Georgia purchased the four-bedroom, three-bathroom home, the garage was large enough for three cars.

After his wife died from cancer more than four years ago, Rollie retired from the police department where he was a homicide detective to stay home and take care of his daughters.

His pension was good, but not good enough, and when his former partner Teal recommended Rollie apply for a private investigator's license and work for lawyers, that is exactly what he did.

Rollie put up a wall with a door and converted the garage into an office. After three years, he had an extensive list of attorneys for clients. Most of the time, the caseload involved background information on witnesses and the occasional surveillance. The money was excellent and the work easy.

But every once in a while, something out of the ordinary came along. During the past summer, a client by the name of Joanna Kearns, on Teal's recommendation, came to Rollie's attention.

Joanna's sister Julia was married to a young attorney named John Knox. Julia worked in Tower One of the original World Trade Center and supposedly died on 9/11 of 2001.

Supposedly.

Rollie accepted the challenge, and after months of intense investigative work and several deadly confrontations, Knox, the front runner for New York Governor, was arrested for murder.

In September and October, Rollie took it easy. A few cases here and there, mostly because he was trying to figure out if there was something between him and Joanna Kearns.

Joanna was forty-nine, a tall and striking brunette. She was intelligent with a good sense of humor and, like Rollie, she was alone after divorcing her cheating husband five years ago.

The problem was that Joanna taught middle school in South Carolina and Rollie lived in New York. On the plus side, the girls really liked her. The minus was the distance between them.

At his desk, Rollie checked emails and returned a few calls. A few minutes before 5:00, Gitter and Schram, a very prestigious criminal defense firm called.

"Rollie, Adam Schram," Schram said.

"Mr. Schram, working kind of late, aren't you?" Rollie said. "It's after five."

"Something came to my attention that I could use your help with," Schram said. "It's more of a civil case, but important to an old friend of the firm. Can you come to the office around eleven tomorrow morning?"

"Tomorrow is Saturday," Rollie said.

"I know," Schram said. "But that old friend of mine is… well, I would appreciate it if you could stop by for an hour, say, around eleven."

"I'll be there," Rollie said.

"Thank you, Rollie. I'll see you at eleven, then," Schram said.

After hanging up with Schram, Rollie went to the kitchen to help the girls with dinner.

"Girls, a client of mine called," Rollie said. "I have to go to the City for a bit tomorrow. Grace, if you take your sisters anywhere while I'm out, call me."

"I will," Grace said.

"How long until dinner's ready?" Rollie said.

"Thirty minutes," Grace said.

"Long enough to take Buddy for one more walk around the block," Rollie said. "Gloria, grab his leash."

"Come on, boy, let's go," Gloria said.

CHAPTER TWO

Gitter and Schram was the premier defense firm in Manhattan. To get in their door, you needed a high six-figure retainer and must be prepared for a seven-figure bill.

Both men were in their sixties, with perfect haircuts and manicured nails; they wore custom-made, Italian suits.

Rollie met them in the conference room.

"Coffee, Rollie?" Schram said.

"I'll take a cup," Rollie said.

They served only Kopi Luwak, which cost ninety dollars a pound. Schram poured.

"We are waiting for Mr. Rose," Schram said.

"Of Rose and Rose," Gitter said. "Have you heard of them?"

"Can't say as I have," Rollie said.

"Civil law is what they practice," Schram said. "Estate wills, inheritances, things like that."

"Mr. Rose Senior passed away some time ago and left the firm to his son," Gitter said.

"And this is about what, exactly?" Rollie said.

"It's best to let Mr. Rose explain the details," Schram said.

"He should be here any moment now," Gitter said.

"You said this is a civil matter—am I to assume you won't be part of it?" Rollie said.

"To a degree," Schram said. "John Henry Rose, Senior, was a close friend of ours. While we never overlapped professionally, he was a fine man and a good friend. His son John Henry Junior took over the firm when his father passed about fifteen years ago."

"John Henry Junior brought to our attention the situation he will explain to you when he arrives, and frankly, we thought of you," Gitter said.

"Not that I don't appreciate all the business you've given me, but what's this about?" Rollie said.

"I'm afraid if we tried to explain it, we'd only botch it up," Schram said.

"By the way, have you heard the latest on Knox?" Gitter said.

"I haven't been following it," Rollie said. "At some point, I'll be called to court to testify, but I haven't had much to do with it lately."

"It appears Knox hired that defense attorney from Texas, the one with a ponytail who wears cowboy clothes," Gitter said. "By the time Knox is sentenced, he'll be penniless and facing twenty-five years."

The office door opened and Rose entered, carrying a large briefcase. He was a squirrelly little man in his sixties, with snow-white hair, blue eyes, and he wore rimless glasses.

"Sorry for the delay, the subway ran late," Rose said.

"Mr. Rose, this is Rollie Finch," Schram said.

"Very impressive work on the Knox case," Rose said. "Coffee, please."

Gitter filled a cup for Rose, who sat beside Rollie at the table.

Rose took a sip and said, "Now then, what have you told Mr. Finch?"

"Not much," Schram said. "We wouldn't know how to explain it anyway."

Rose looked at Rollie. "Well, let's get started then," he said. "Mr. Finch, I am a civil attorney, as was my father who started the firm. I handle wills, estates, and things of that nature. Are you with me so far?"

"Yes," Rollie said.

"Good," Rose said. "Now then, have you ever heard of a tontine?"

"It's an old European custom where a group of people put money into an account and whoever is the last person left alive claims the pot," Rollie said.

"Yes, that is exactly right," Rose said. "Now, sixty years ago, one hundred people of Romanian descent started a tontine through my father. Each person or family put five thousand dollars into a bank account that was overseen by my father."

"That's five hundred thousand dollars," Rollie said.

"And worth just north of twelve million today," Rose said. "The reason I am telling you this is that one man, eighty-six-year-old Victor Enache, is the last person still alive of the original one hundred investors."

"A long wait, but good for him," Rollie said.

"Yes, but there is a problem," Rose said. "Since my father passed some fifteen years ago, I have kept records on every individual, and there are six members that I can't account for one hundred percent."

"How so?" Rollie said.

"They've disappeared," Rose said. "Vanished under mysterious circumstances. I can't, in good faith, release the funds to Mr. Enache if other members are still alive."

"And so you need me to do what, exactly?" Rollie said.

"Look into the six unaccounted for so I can determine if Mr. Enache gets the funds or not," Rose said. "Police reports are sketchy at best, and I don't feel comfortable releasing the money if there is any possibility that any of them are living."

"Is there some time limit in place?" Rollie said.

"No binding limit, but Enache *is* eighty-six years old," Rose said.

"I'll look into the missing six," Rollie said. "Who pays my bill?"

"I've allocated funds from the tontine account," Rose said.

"My standard fee is a hundred and fifty per hour, plus expenses," Rollie said. "I will let you know what I need for expenses after I review the reports on the missing six. Is that agreeable to you, Mr. Rose?"

"Yes, quite," Rose said.

"I didn't bring my standard contract with me, but I can…" Rollie said.

"We have some on file," Gitter said. "I'll get one."

A few minutes later, Rose and Rollie signed his standard contract and Gitter made a copy for Rose.

"I'll call your office on Monday after I've had a chance to review the files you left me," Rollie said.

"Fine. Now I have another appointment, so if you'll excuse me," Rose said.

After Rose left, Rollie said, "How about another cup of coffee?"

Schram refilled three cups.

"This doesn't sound too complicated," Gitter said. "At least it's not a criminal case."

"Speaking of which, we may have something for you in a few weeks, once you're done with this tontine business," Schram said.

"I don't think it will take too long," Rollie said.

"Thanks for helping out an old friend," Schram said.

"Thanks for the twelve-dollar cup of coffee," Rollie replied.

CHAPTER THREE

As he drove home along Queens Boulevard, Grace called him on his cell phone.

"Dad, we're taking Buddy to the dog park, but we're walking," she said.

"Okay, sweetheart, I'll see you when I get home," Rollie said.

As he neared the house, Rollie decided to drive to the dog park first, which was located just six blocks away.

He parked on a side street, grabbed a coffee from the deli on Queens Boulevard, and then found a bench at the dog park.

As fall days went, today was one of the best. The temperature topped out at sixty and the sun was shining.

The girls were playing Frisbee with Buddy. The beagle puppy had boundless energy as he chased the red disc and returned it to the girls.

Rollie was lucky in that his daughters genuinely loved each other. The age differences seemed not to matter. That love came from their mother early on and stuck with them.

Finally, Buddy had had enough, and the girls walked him to the bench.

"Hey, Dad," Grace said.

"Want a lift home?" Rollie said.

"Buddy could use it," Gloria said.

"Car's across the street," Rollie said.

.   .   .

Rollie changed into comfortable sweats and went to his office in the garage. Against the back wall was a step climber and beside that a Bowflex home gym. He did thirty minutes on each and then grabbed a shower. He changed into slacks and a sweatshirt, and found the girls in the kitchen, doing homework at the table.

Grace excelled at math, Giselle at science. Gloria was an all-around good student. Buddy was beside Gloria's legs, taking a nap.

Rollie grabbed a can of ginger ale from the fridge. "I'd like to get dinner going around six," he said.

"We'll be done," Grace said.

Rollie went to his office, sat at his desk, and opened the thick file Rose had given him.

The first name in the file was Andrel Barbu. If he were still alive, he would be eighty-one years old. He was a barber with his own shop in the Bronx for forty-seven years. His wife died eleven years ago, after which he sold the shop and retired to a small condo in Bronxville, a small town in Westchester County.

Barbu's three children were scattered across the country and he was living alone at the time he disappeared seventeen months ago.

Barbu had enjoyed good health and belonged to a mall walker's club. Every morning at 8:30, club members would meet at the Westchester Mall where security would let them in and they would walk the interior for one hour. Afterward, many in the club would go for coffee at the food court in the mall.

After he didn't show up for five morning walks, members in the club thought Barbu might be ill and they decided to check on him. They went to his condo and when he didn't answer the door, they went to the police.

The police locksmith let two detectives into Barbu's condo where they did a thorough search, found nothing disturbed, and after twenty-four hours, contacted his children.

Barbu went down in the books as a missing person and has never been heard from since.

Rollie read the detective's reports. No one in Barbu's condo building could pinpoint the last time they saw him, although nearly everyone in the building knew about his morning walks at the mall.

Barbu's three children inherited his belongings, a small insurance policy, and his life savings.

And the book was closed on Andrel Barbu.

Marco Cazacu was seventy-seven when he disappeared fourteen months ago. It was actually Marco's father who had paid the five thousand to join the tontine, but he died shortly afterward, and then Marco took control.

Cazacu worked for the New York City Transit Authority as a motorman and spent forty-three years driving trains around Brooklyn, Manhattan, Queens and the Bronx. He retired at sixty-five with an excellent pension and benefits.

He never married and after he retired, he moved to a retirement community on Staten Island. He purchased a one-bedroom condo, still drove his car, and was in excellent health.

He'd joined a golfing group that played three times a week at the retirement community course and after several years, became an excellent golfer. One day in June, he didn't show up for tee-time. His group thought he might be ill and went to his condo to check on him. His car was in its designated spot, but Cazacu wasn't home.

They called the community campus police, who did a search of Cazacu's condo. Nothing was out of place, and except for Cazacu, nothing appeared to be missing.

After twenty-four hours, Staten Island detectives wrote it up as a missing person's case. Fourteen months later, Cazacu was still missing. Some family members, cousins and nephews, made inquiries but to no avail.

German and Turkish on his mother's side, George Wendt wasn't Romanian, but his wife was, so she signed into the tontine for him. Wendt was thirty-one when he invested in the tontine, and would be five years older than Victor Enache—if Wendt hadn't vanished twelve months ago.

Wendt and his wife left New York shortly after investing in the tontine and moved to Maine where he became a lobster fisherman. By the time he was forty, Wendt had three boats and thousands of traps. Wendt and his wife had one son, and when Wendt reached the age of sixty, he retired and turned the business over to George Junior, but kept half the profits.

Wendt's wife died suddenly at the age of eighty from a stroke, so Wendt moved to Key Largo to a retirement community to live out the rest of his days. Almost a year after that, his son George Jr. went missing from a lobster boat during a January storm off the coast of Maine.

Still blessed with great health and strength, Wendt had become an active member of the retirement community, until one day in late October, he was gone without a trace.

The retirement community police investigated and then turned it over to the county sheriff's department, where detectives declared it a missing person's case.

Tamas Lupu was eighty-four when he vanished one day from his retirement home in South Carolina. Tamas, after a two-year stint in the Army, joined the New York City Fire Department where he put in forty years, and then retired comfortably at age sixty-four. His wife of fifty years died when he was seventy-five, a few years after they'd moved to a retirement community on Shore Island off the South Carolina coast.

Island security investigated Lupu's disappearance and then called the county sheriff's department, who declared it a missing person's case. That was in August of last year.

Dennis Reiter was eighty-one when he vanished from a nursing home in Providence, Rhode Island. A steel worker, Reiter had an accident on a job site and fell twenty feet to a platform and broke his back. He lived, but never walked again. He was fifty-five at the time of the accident.

Reiter never married and though he was confined to a wheelchair, he was very active and sociable. Financially he was comfortable, having received a large sum of money from the insurance payout. In addition, Reiter received social security.

One morning while he was sitting in the back gardens of the nursing home—something he did nearly every morning from spring to fall—Reiter simply disappeared.

After failing to locate Reiter anywhere on site, police were called. Twenty-four hours later, Reiter became another missing person's report.

William Waite was the youngest member of the tontine to disappear. He was Polish and Romanian, with his mother being Romanian. She entered the tontine when William was just six years old. His father died at the age of forty from alcoholism. His mother died at the age of eighty, but before she died, she turned her tontine membership over to William.

Waite never married and fashioned himself a lady's man of sorts, romancing older women and fleecing them as he went along.

He was sixty-six years old and living in Manhattan when he disappeared six months ago. At the time of his disappearance, he was making a living as a companion to wealthy widows in their seventies and eighties. He was living in a one-bedroom apartment on 74th Street and Riverside Drive when he just vanished. Several of the women he was supposed to escort to various events called the police when they were unable to locate him.

Officers had the building maintenance man let them into his apartment. Everything was intact; nothing was missing except for Waite.

They turned it over to detectives.

After twenty-four hours, NYPD listed him as a missing person.

Rollie had read enough. He didn't try to digest the information or make notes. He would do that tomorrow.

It was nearly six o'clock, so he headed to the kitchen to help the girls prepare the evening meal.

They had finished their homework.

"What shall we do for dinner?" Rollie said.

CHAPTER FOUR

On Sunday morning after breakfast, Rollie went to his office and read through Rose's documents again, this time, making notes on a legal pad.

It was obvious that someone was systematically removing the surviving members of the one hundred participants in the tontine.

Eighty-six-year-old Victor Enoch stood to gain the twelve million if it could be proven that he is the last surviving member, but was he capable of taking out the six other members at his age?

Rollie scribbled a note. *Find out about Victor Enoch from Rose. Enoch's history, medical condition, where he lives.*

In any murder investigation, it always comes down to who would benefit the most by committing the murder.

In this case, it pointed to Victor Enoch.

Sixty-six-year-old William Waite would be the primary suspect if it weren't for the fact that he was one of the missing six.

He needed to meet with Rose on Monday.

Rollie changed into comfortable sweats, and then did thirty minutes on the step-climber and thirty minutes on the Bowflex.

After a quick shower and change of clothes, he stopped by the kitchen for a mug of coffee where the girls were hunched around Grace's laptop.

"And we're doing…?" Rollie said.

"Looking for part-time jobs," Grace said.

"We're always bugging you for money, Dad," Giselle said.

"Right now, your job is to do well in school and need money," Rollie said. "My job is to make sure you do well in school and supply the money you need."

"For food, clothing and shelter," Grace said. "We'd like to earn our own pin money, Dad."

"Well, you're eighteen now and Giselle is sixteen, so a part-time job might do you some good," Rollie said. "But you should be aware of the pitfalls."

"Pitfalls?" Grace said.

"Of which there are many," Rollie said. "When you work, you have a responsibility to your employer. You also have a responsibility to school. On top of that, you have a responsibility to me. You have to do well by your employer, maintain your grades in school, and still do your part around the house. If one slips, they all slip. Understand?"

"We get it, Dad," Grace said.

"So, what are you looking at?" Rollie said.

"There are several part-time openings at the pet store where we buy Buddy's food," Grace said.

"We'd like to apply," Giselle said.

"What are the hours?" Rollie said.

"Four to seven on Monday, Wednesday and Friday, and from noon to five on Saturday," Grace said.

"Now explain to me how that changes the dynamics of our household," Rollie said.

Grace and Giselle stared at Rollie.

"What Dad means is…" Gloria said.

"We know what he means," Grace said.

"Then explain it to me," Rollie said.

"Well, on Monday, Wednesday and Friday, we need to make sure Gloria is home right after school so we can be on time at the pet store," Grace said.

"Also, we'll be eating later on the days we work," Grace said.

"And doing our homework when we'd normally be watching TV," Giselle said.

"And?" Rollie said.

Grace and Giselle stared at Rollie again.

"I think what Dad means is, what if he's working and not home on the days you guys are working at the store," Gloria said. "I'm only fourteen and not supposed to be left alone."

"Oh," Grace said.

"That's a big oh," Rollie said. "However, I do have a solution, if Mrs. Kravitz is willing to come over and stay with Gloria on the days I'm out."

"Can you ask her?" Grace said.

"I can, but I think it should come from you," Rollie said.

"Let's go," Grace said to Giselle.

After Grace and Giselle walked over to Mrs. Kravitz's house, Gloria said, "Why am I always left out?"

"You're not left out, you're just younger," Rollie said.

"They get to have a job and I have to stay poor," Gloria said.

"Poor?" Rollie said.

"You know what I mean, Dad," Gloria said.

"Indeed, I do," Rollie said. "And I am prepared to up your allowance substantially for services rendered."

"Dad, speak English," Gloria said.

"On Monday, Wednesday and Friday and to a degree on Saturday, you and I are the primary chefs for dinner," Rollie said. "So, for that and other chores your sisters won't be around to do, you get a substantial raise in your allowance."

"Cool," Gloria said with a grin.

Grace and Giselle returned. "Mrs. Kravitz said she would be delighted to," Grace said.

"She actually said that, delighted," Giselle said.

"Come on, Gloria, let's take Buddy to the park," Rollie said.

"What about us?" Grace said.

Rollie looked at his watch. "If you hurry, you can get to the pet store and apply for jobs before it closes," Rollie said.

• • •

Rollie sat on a bench in the dog park and watched as Grace and Buddy visited with friends and their dogs.

Buddy was super-friendly and, in turn, made friends easily.

In his shirt pocket, Rollie's cell phone rang. He checked the number and said, "Hi, Joanna."

"Hi, Rollie," Joanna said. "I have a bit of news for you and the girls."

"Good news, I hope," Rollie said.

"You asked me if I could make it for Thanksgiving and the answer is yes, I can," Joanna said.

"Great news," Rollie said. "I'll tell the girls at dinner tonight."

"I think I'm going to fly, though," Joanna said. "Seven hours in a car each way is a real pain."

"No worries, we'll pick you up at the airport," Rollie said.

"We'll have a lot to talk about," Joanna said.

"Yes, we will," Rollie said.

"Okay then, I'll talk to you later," Joanna said.

• • •

At dinner, Grace and Giselle were bubbling over with news about their part-time jobs.

"Mr. Fudderman said we both have jobs," Giselle said.

"Minimum wage, but we can get raises after ninety days," Gloria said.

"Thirteen-fifty-an-hour to start is nothing to sneeze at," Rollie said.

"So, what are you guys going to be doing?" Gloria said.

"Feeding animals, cleaning out cages, helping customers and ringing the register," Grace said.

"And working in the stockroom," Giselle added.

"We start our training tomorrow," Grace said,

"Very good," Rollie said. "And I have some news of my own. Joanna has accepted our invitation to Thanksgiving dinner."

After five minutes of non-stop talking, the girls quieted down enough for Rollie to get a word in edgewise.

"We have three weeks to prepare, but in the meantime, I have some work to do in the morning," Rollie said. "If I'm not back by three thirty, Gloria, get Buddy and head over to Mrs. Kravitz until I get home. And call me."

"I will," Gloria said.

"And Grace, you wait until Gloria is with Mrs. Kravitz," Rollie said.

"No problem, Dad," Grace said.

"Whose turn is it to do the dishes?" Rollie said.

Grace looked at the chart on the refrigerator. "Yours," she said.

CHAPTER FIVE

"Thank you for seeing me on such short notice," Rollie said as he took a chair opposite Mr. Rose's desk.

Rose's office was on the first floor of his townhouse on West 8th Avenue on the fringe of the Village.

The office was a cluttered mess, and the furniture looked like it belonged to Rose's father from fifty years ago.

"I have a family coming by at noon for a will reading, so how can I help you?" Rose said.

"I'd like to find out what happened to the six men on the list," Rollie said.

"Isn't that why you were hired?" Rose said.

"Yes, but I mean, I want to really delve into this," Rollie said. "I believe, after what I've read, that the six men were murdered for the tontine money and that changes this dramatically."

"I knew you were going to say that," Rose said. "But I don't handle criminal cases, as you know."

"But Gitter and Schram do," Rollie said.

"I see," Rose said. "Before we talk about that, first, establish the fact of murder."

"Exactly why I'm here," Rollie said. "I need expense money in order to do that."

"How much?"

"Twenty thousand to start, more if needed," Rollie said.

"Can you come back around two thirty?" Rose said. "I'll need to withdraw funds before my next appointment."

"No problem," Rollie said.

"If these six men were murdered as you suspect, then by whom?" Rose said.

"That's what I intend to find out," Rollie said.

•   •   •

"So, why are you in town, what do you want, and why are you taking me to lunch?" Police Captain Bill Teal asked as he and Rollie took seats at Teal's favorite diner.

"I can't stop by to see my close friend and ex-partner and take him to lunch without having a hidden agenda?" Rollie said.

"No," Teal said. "I know better."

"Truth is I'm working a new case, I needed to be in the City, and I have some time to kill," Rollie said. "I thought you might like to grab some lunch."

Teal bit into a thick, juicy bacon-cheeseburger and said, "You know, my wife watches my cholesterol like a hawk watches baby mice."

"A burger instead of carrot sticks and lettuce leaves every day isn't going to kill you," Rollie said.

"So, what's this new case about?" Teal said.

"A civil matter, at the moment," Rollie said, "involving some missing persons."

"Sounds exciting," Teal said. "Only not. I got my notice to appear in court on the Knox case. Did you?"

"Not yet," Rollie said.

"How did Andrews take it when you turned him down again?" Teal said.

Andrews was the Chief of Police and he wanted Rollie to return to the department as Assistant Chief of Detectives.

"He understands family comes first," Rollie said.

"Good."

"So how are things going between you and Joanna?" Teal said.

"Way too soon to tell," Rollie said. "She did agree to Thanksgiving dinner, so we'll see."

"Holidays are important in a relationship," Teal said. "My wife is planning a turkey made from tofu."

"Jesus," Rollie said.

"Let's get some dessert," Teal said. "I can't look at one more carrot stick."

• • •

Rose handed Rollie a thick envelope that contained $20,000. "Please get receipts, as I have to account to the tontine fund," Rose said.

"That's the only way I operate," Rollie said.

"So, what are your suspicions?" Rose said.

"It's too soon to form an educated opinion, but it appears on the surface that someone is systematically removing surviving members of the tontine," Rollie said. "It could be a surviving member we're unaware of at the moment, or it could be one of the six has faked his disappearance and has removed the other five."

"That would make Mr. Enache a target?" Rose said.

"It would if it proves to be true," Rollie said. "And as a precaution, it wouldn't hurt to check on Enache and let him know what's happening."

"I shall do that," Rose said.

"I'll update you as things progress," Rollie said.

"Don't forget receipts," Rose said.

.   .   .

Rollie arrived home at 4:00 and walked over to pick up Gloria and Buddy at Mrs. Kravitz's house.

While he was driving home, Grace had called to let him know they were taking Gloria next door.

"Have a lot of homework?" Rollie said.

"Gags," Gloria said.

"Well, you can go home and get started, or we can take Buddy to the dog park for an hour," Rollie said. "Choice is yours."

"I'll get his leash," Gloria said.

CHAPTER SIX

While Grace did her homework, Rollie went to his office and read his notes.

It made sense to arrange things geographically rather than by a timeline.

That put William Waite in Manhattan at the top of the list. Andrel Barbu in Bronxville was next, followed by Marco Cazacu in Staten Island. Dennis Reiter in Providence was fourth, followed by Tamas Lupu in South Carolina, leaving George Wendt in Florida for last.

Rollie decided to tackle Waite tomorrow morning, and if there was time, shoot north to Bronxville.

He went to the kitchen where Gloria was just finishing up.

"Your sisters should be home around seven fifteen," Rollie said. "So, I'll start dinner at six thirty."

"I'm done with my homework. Can I take Buddy in the backyard for half an hour?" Gloria said.

"I'll go with you," Rollie said.

Rollie grabbed a can of ginger ale from the fridge and sat at the patio table while Gloria worked with Buddy on learning tricks. For each command Gloria gave him, Buddy was rewarded with a treat.

People don't just vanish into thin air without someone behind the vanishing act, Rollie thought.

Waite was a career gigolo who preyed on older women for money. Maybe there was a jealous husband lurking behind door number one? Or a relative of granny who killed him before he could fleece granny out of her life savings? Or someone who didn't want him to inherit the tontine money.

Andrel Barbu in Bronxville was just a thirty-minute drive from Manhattan. If Rollie finished up with Waite early enough, he would tackle Barbu. Even though Barbu was eighty-one, he was in excellent shape and a mall walker, so somebody didn't want to chance him living another decade, and made him disappear. He was a barber, so how many enemies could he have besides someone in the tontine?

Marco Cazacu was another story entirely. A working man all his life, an excellent pension, a retirement home on Staten Island, a man who never married and liked to play golf. He probably would have made it to ninety and was eliminated for the twelve million. Since traveling to Staten Island was an all-day affair, Rollie would devote an entire day to Cazacu.

Dennis Reiter in Providence was another all-day affair, so he was fourth on the list. Crippled and confined to a wheelchair for thirty years, he might have lived another ten, so he was likely eliminated to keep him from collecting the tontine.

Tamas Lupu in South Carolina required a plane ride, which Rollie didn't mind, as it gave him a reason to see Joanna before Thanksgiving. A career fireman, a widower, Lupu was eighty-four when he vanished.

Last on the list was George Wendt. Wendt was ninety when he disappeared from Florida, but healthy, strong, and comfortable, financially. A widower, someone didn't want to chance him reaching a hundred.

"Gloria, let's get dinner going."

While Rollie breaded six large chicken breasts, Gloria peeled potatoes. "Should we make carrots or corn with the mashed potatoes?" she said.

"I vote corn," Rollie said.

"Me, too."

"So, since your sisters aren't here, we'll go with corn," Rollie said.

Once the potatoes and corn were done and set aside, Grace said, "The siblings won't be home for forty-five minutes, can we play a video game?"

"I don't see why not," Rollie said. "Let me set the timer on the oven."

For thirty minutes, Rollie tried to keep up with Gloria as she beat the pants off him in a game called Winds of War.

When the timer sounded in the kitchen, Gloria stood up. "I better set the table," she said.

By the time Grace and Giselle came through the front door, the table was set, and dinner was ready.

Talk around the table was about the pet store and the first day on the job.

"I cleaned out a dozen cages and stocked shelves all afternoon," Giselle said.

Rollie looked at Grace. "And you?"

"Helped customers find stuff and rang on a register," Grace said. "Mr. Fudderman said he was happy with both of us."

"Good," Rollie said. "What's your schedule look like?"

"Wednesday, Friday, and Saturday from noon to five," Grace said.

"OK, well, I'll be working tomorrow, so you guys stay put when you get home," Rollie said. "You can go to the dog park if you don't have too much homework."

"Okay, Dad," Grace said.

"Gloria and I will do the dishes so you two can get to it," Rollie said.

"Dad, after the dishes, can we take Buddy for a walk?" Gloria said.

"Sure," Rollie said.

Once the dishes were done, Rollie and Gloria took Buddy for a long stroll around the block.

Halfway through, Rollie asked, "Why so quiet?"

"I don't know," Gloria said. "I think… never mind."

"Feeling left out, huh?" Rollie said.

"A little. I guess," Gloria said.

"That happens sometimes to the youngest," Rollie said. "And seeing as how you can't make yourself any older, you just have to wait your turn."

"That's not very comforting," Gloria said.

"Maybe not, but think of all the extra allowance money you're earning," Rollie said.

"Yeah," Gloria said and smiled. "Yeah."

CHAPTER SEVEN

Rollie lucked out and found a vacant parking space on the street on 74th and Riverside.

William Waite's building was pure Riverside Drive: expensive, complete with doorman. As Rollie approached the building, the doorman looked him over.

Rollie removed his wallet from his jacket pocket and held it open for the doorman to read his identification.

"Good morning," Rollie said.

"Private investigator, huh?" the doorman said. "I was on the job for twenty-five years in the Bronx and Brooklyn myself. You?"

"Twenty-three in Manhattan," Rollie said. "The last ten in Homicide."

"Who are you here to see?" the doorman said.

"William Waite," Rollie said.

"The cops already closed the books on him," the doorman said.

"I know, but this is a private matter," Rollie said. "What can you tell me about him?"

"Same as I told the detective six months ago," the doorman said. "Waite was an old gigolo who took old ladies for their money. Everybody in the building knew it. Sometimes he came home with a seventy-five-year-old woman on his arm, other times one would show up in her limo. He had a talent, that guy, for fleecing them but good."

"Do you know how long he lived here?" Rollie said.

"A long time, something like thirty years," the doorman said. "His apartment was the last of the rent controlled in the building. He was paying $1,400 a month for Riverside Drive. Any new tenant pays $3,500 a month."

"So, what happened to him?" Rollie said.

"You tell me," the doorman said. "One day he just wasn't here."

"How did people in the building become aware that he was gone?" Rollie asked.

"Some old women showed up when he didn't answer his phone," the doorman said. "They thought he stood them up for some social functions. The building manager used his pass key to check his place and the man just wasn't there."

"How many doormen are working here and what are their hours?" Rollie said.

"There are four regulars and two backups," the doorman said. "I work six a.m. to two p.m., then my relief comes on at two and leaves at ten. After that, a tenant has to use their own key to get in."

"So, he could have left anywhere between ten at night and six in the morning and not be seen?" Rollie said.

"Sure," the doorman said.

"Is there a service entrance for trash removal and deliveries?" Rollie said.

"The alleyway over there, but only the superintendent and building manager have a key to that door," the doorman said.

"Is it classified a fire door?" Rollie said.

"Yeah."

"Then it's only locked from the outside," Rollie said.

"True, but if Waite wanted to disappear, why use the service elevator?" the doorman said. "All he'd have to do is wait until ten o'clock."

"Ever talk to him?" Rollie asked.

"Hello, goodbye, how ya doing, can you get me a cab?" the doorman said.

"What about his friends?" Rollie said.

"What friends, unless you count his string of old ladies," the doorman said.

"Do you remember who the detective was who investigated?" Rollie said.

"Art something or another from the twentieth," the doorman said.

"Thanks," Rollie said.

"Hey, cop-to-cop, what's this about?" the doorman said.

"Waite stood to inherit a great deal of money," Rollie said.

"Bummer," the doorman said.

Rollie returned to his car and drove to the twentieth precinct about ten blocks away and parked in the visitor's lot. He entered the station house and stopped at the desk.

"Lieutenant Rollie Finch to see Detective Art Chapman," Rollie said.

The desk sergeant called the squad room and Chapman met Rollie at the desk.

"Rollie, it's been years," Chapman said as they shook hands.

"Can you spare ten minutes?" Rollie said.

They went to the squad room where Chapman sat behind his desk and Rollie took a chair.

"I heard you retired after your wife passed away," Chapman said.

Rollie nodded. "I'm working as a private investigator these days, mostly for lawyers," he said.

"Gumshoes and bars," Chapman said.

That was an inside joke referencing how many retired cops become private detectives or open a bar.

"So, what do you need?" Chapman said.

"Information on a William Waite, a missing person from six months ago," Rollie said.

Chapman tapped keys on his computer. "Vanished from his apartment on Riverside Drive," he said. "What about him?"

"Anything you can tell me," Rollie said.

"Two women showed up at his apartment when he stood them up for some social functions," Chapman said. "The manager checked his apartment and then called us. I did a check of his place and it was neat as a pin. No dirty dishes in the sink, bed made, no dust on anything and no signs of forced entry or a struggle."

"His finances?" Rollie said.

"The guy did alright for an old gigolo," Chapman said. "Had $200,000 in Chase Manhattan, another $100,000 in a stock portfolio, ten large in a checking account and was also collecting $1,500 a month from Social security."

"His rent money," Rollie said. "Any follow up?"

"I tried locating relatives, friends and even spoke with the two women who called it in," Chapman said. "The guy just up and vanished."

"Hospital and police reports?" Rollie said.

"Nothing," Chapman said. "But I will tell you this. If he took off on his own, he took nothing with him. No luggage, not a stitch of clothing and I put an alert on the bank to notify me if his accounts are used and so far, nothing."

"Thanks, Art," Rollie said.

"So, what's this about, Rollie?" Chapman said.

"Wait was in line to inherit a great deal of money," Rollie said.

"Bummer," Chapman said.

•　　•　　•

Rollie drove north on the FDR to Bronxville in Westchester County. Bronxville was actually a village inside the town of Eastchester, and a wealthy little village at that.

Barbu's barbershop had served him well if he retired to Bronxville. Before proceeding to Barbu's condo, Rollie stopped at a diner for some lunch.

He grabbed a copy of the local newspaper, sat at the counter, and ordered a bowl of chili and a glass of ginger ale.

Barbu's condo was in a gated community with a security hut and a gate. Rollie stopped to talk to the security guard on duty.

The first thing Rollie did was show his identification to the guard. "No kidding," he said. "I did twenty-two with Yonkers PD. You?"

"Twenty-three with NYPD," Rollie said.

"No kidding. So, what brings you here?"

"Andrel Barbu," Rollie said.

"He was a peach of an old man," the security guard said. "What about him?"

"I've been hired to investigate his disappearance," Rollie said.

"The police already did that."

"This is for a civil matter," Rollie said. "Anything you can tell me would be appreciated."

"He was already living here when I took the job a few years ago," the security guard said, "He was a barber and had six chairs. He must have done alright to afford living here. You know, almost every morning he would drive to the mall and walk the interior with a mall walker club. He was in great shape, that old man."

"Did he have any enemies you know of?" Rollie said.

"Him?" the security guard said. "Let me tell you about him. Every Sunday, any man who lives here could go to his condo between noon and six and get a free haircut."

"Can I see the manager?" Rollie said.

"I'll call him on the phone, see if he's in."

•   •   •

"It was the mall walkers that first alerted me Mr. Barbu was missing," the complex manager said. "I called the police, and they brought a locksmith to enter his condo. From what I saw the place was neat and tidy. His car was in its assigned spot, so whatever happened I never found out."

"Reports say it was five days when the mall walkers first noticed he wasn't there before the police entered his condo," Rollie said.

"That sounds about right," the complex manager said.

"What about his furniture and clothing?" Rollie asked.

"We have a large storage unit for unclaimed belongings from people who died."

"Do you remember the detective who investigated?" Rollie said.

The complex manager opened a drawer and removed a folder and scanned it. "Detective Ronald Voit," he said.

"Thanks for your time," Rollie said.

"I don't mean to pry into someone else's business, but what's this about?" the complex manager said.

"Barbu was in line to inherit a large sum of money," Rollie said.

"Wow. That's a real…"

"Bummer," Rollie said.

•   •   •

"I went through his entire condo and found nothing suspicious," Detective Voit said. "Nothing appeared to be missing; no sign of a struggle and all his clothing and luggage was intact. Hell, even his car was in place."

"Did you contact his three children?"

"I did and all they did was fight over his will," Voit said. "The man did alright for himself as a barber. He had $350,000 in cash and stocks and an insurance policy of $500,000 with his three children as beneficiaries. As far as I know, it's still in the hands of the courts about the condo."

"Anybody see him leave his condo before he disappeared?" Rollie said.

"I interviewed everybody in his building," Voit said. "They all go to bed early and nobody saw or heard a thing. I spoke with his mall walkers club and he was fine one day and not there the next."

"Thank you, detective, for your time," Rollie said.

"Mind me asking why you're interested," Voit said.

"Mr. Barbu stood to inherit a great deal of money," Rollie said.

"That's…" Voit said.

"A bummer," Rollie said.

"Unfortunate," Voit said.

"That, too."

•   •   •

Access to William Waite's Riverside Drive apartment between 10 p.m. and 6 a.m. when doormen were not on duty made him easily accessible to kidnapping. Anybody who kept watch on Waite could learn his late-night habits and grab him when a doorman wasn't on duty after dark when Riverside Drive is dark and deserted.

Andrel Barbu's condo disappearance—another matter. A guard was on duty 24-7. Barbu was vulnerable when he drove to the mall to walk with the club, but his car was still in its allotted space.

Rollie flipped through documents on Barbu. The mall walkers reported him missing on a Thursday after not seeing him since

Sunday morning.

Sunday. The day Barbu gave haircuts to male residents in the complex for free.

Barbu gave a haircut to his kidnapper.

That required surveillance, an access in and out and perfect timing.

Rollie closed his notebook and went to the kitchen where the girls were doing their homework. He looked at the schedule of household chores taped to the refrigerator. "Grace, it's our turn to make dinner tonight," he said.

"I checked," Grace said. "We'll be done with our homework by five thirty."

"Okay," Rollie said and went to his bedroom to change into sweats. He returned to the office where he did thirty minutes on the step climber and another thirty on the Bowflex.

Two men on the same list of potential tontine inheritors disappear under mysterious circumstances from vastly different places. A wealthy section of Manhattan and a condo complex in Bronxville, located about twenty miles apart.

Somebody put in the time.

After his workout, Rollie took a shower and changed into comfortable sweats and returned to the kitchen.

"Okay, Grace, let's get dinner started," he said.

CHAPTER EIGHT

The ride to Staten Island was long and tedious. Rollie took the BQE into Brooklyn and then drove to the Verrazzano-Narrows Bridge to Staten Island. Once on Staten Island, he drove to the retirement community where Marco Cazacu lived and had disappeared from.

The retirement community was large, eighty homes, a gold course and tennis courts and a community center that was spread out across 500 acres, of which the golf course took up one hundred and fifty.

But it wasn't gated.

Rollie drove into the complex on the main road that circumvented the entire grounds, all eighty homes, golf courts, tennis courts and community center.

He parked in front of a home that served as the manager's office for the complex.

A woman was behind a desk when Rollie walked in and showed his identification. "Are you the complex manager?" he said.

"No, I'm the office manger," the woman said. "Mrs. Thompson is the manager."

"May I see her?" Rollie said.

"Let me check."

The woman left her desk and walked down a hallway. She

returned a minute later. "Follow me, please," she said.

The woman led Rollie to an office where Mrs. Thompson sat behind a desk. She was a plump woman in her fifties who spoke with a Brooklyn accent.

Rollie showed her his identification.

"What can I do for you, Mr. Finch?" Mrs. Thompson said. "You're certainly not old enough to live here."

"I've been hired to look into the disappearance of Marco Cazacu," Rollie said.

"Why, Mr. Cazacu disappeared fourteen months ago," Mrs. Thompson said.

"We know, but it's important to the people who hired me to take another look," Rollie said.

"Well, what do you want to know?"

"Tell me about Mr. Cazacu," Rollie said.

"He was a very popular man," Mrs. Thompson said. "Played a lot of golf and cards at the community center. He was reported missing by his golfing group and me and security went to his home to check and he wasn't there. I called the police and they investigated, and they listed him as a missing person. That's all I know."

"How many security people do you employ?" Rollie asked.

"Two from eight in the morning until midnight, then one overnight."

"I noticed a lack of security cameras on the streets," Rollie said.

"Every year we put it to a vote and every year the residents reject it," Mrs. Thompson said. "They claim it makes them feel like they live in a fishbowl."

"Are there a lot of incidents here?" Rollie said.

"If you mean crime, the answer is no," Mrs. Thompson said. "For the most part our security calls are medical related."

"Where is the golf course from here?" Rollie said.

"I'll run you over," Mrs. Thompson said. "We keep the course open until the first snow."

Mrs. Thompson took Rollie to the golf course in a golf cart. The grass was still green, the temperature neared sixty degrees and residents were out in force on the greens.

The ride from the office to the course took seven minutes.

"It's a long walk for some of these people," Rollie said.

"The course manager and his staff will pick them up if they reserve a tee-time and bring them back afterward," Mrs. Thompson said. "Some who are closer and able, choose to walk."

"I'd like to see the course manager if I may," Rollie said.

"Mr. Cazacu was one of the good ones alright," the course manager said when Mrs. Thompson escorted Rollie to the course office.

"Did he ever take a cart from his house to the course?" Rollie said.

"Every time," the course manager said. "He had a bum right knee."

"What was his usual time?" Rollie said.

"Eight o'clock," the course manager said. "A cart would pick him up around seven forty-five."

"How many staff do you have?"

"Four."

"Thank you for your time," Rollie said.

Driving back to the office, Rollie said, "Would you remember the name of the responding detective?"

"No, but I'm sure it's in the paperwork," Mrs. Thompson said.

•   •   •

Sergeant Cole of the 122nd precinct handed Rollie a mug of coffee and then sat behind his desk.

"Yeah, I remember Mr. Cazacu because it was so odd the way he disappeared," Cole said. "Without a trace. I checked his entire house and found nothing out of place and he was a good housekeeper."

"Family?"

"Couldn't find a one," Cole said. "Alive, anyway."

"Finances?"

"Solid. Money in the bank. A great pension, but if kidnapping was the idea a ransom note or call never came forward."

"Hospitals?"

"Checked and rechecked. Same with other departments on SI and the boroughs," Cole said. "Now why don't you tell me why the interest in a fourteen-month-old missing person's case."

"Mr. Cazacu was on a short list to inherit a great deal of money," Rollie said.

"That's..."

"Unfortunate," Rollie said.

"I was going to say a bummer," Cole said.

"That, too," Rollie said.

·   ·   ·

With some surveillance, it wouldn't be difficult at all to discover Cazacu's habits and golfing routine. Lack of CCTV cameras made it a breeze to steal a golf cart from the course and pick Cazacu up for his tee-time.

Drive him to a parked car, dump him in the trunk and simply drive off the complex.

Rollie lowered his pen and thought for a moment. Three men with predictable habits all disappeared within months of each other. Three men who stood to inherit $12,000,000 if they lived.

In Homicide, when investigating a murder, Rollie always considered who had the most to gain.

In the case of the missing six, it pointed to Victor Enache. Could an eighty-six-year-old man have the guile, strength and stamina needed to plan and carry out such a task?

Rollie used the hard-line phone on his desk to call Rose.

"Mr. Finch, I didn't expect to hear from you so soon," Rose said.

"I'll have a full report for you in ten days or so, but I have a question," Rollie said. "Can you arrange for me to meet with Mr. Enache?"

"I suppose so. Why?"

"As a homicide detective, I don't like loose ends," Rollie said.

"Let me know when and I'll arrange it," Rose said.

"Thanks, I'll let you know," Rollie said.

After hanging up with Rose, Rollie typed his notes as a document in his computer. He read it a few times and then closed the document and went to the kitchen to check on the girls.

"We're just about done with our homework," Grace said.

Rollie looked at the schedule on the refrigerator door. "Grace, you and Giselle are making dinner tonight," he said. "Gloria, when you're ready we'll take Buddy for a walk."

"I'm ready, Dad," Gloria said.

"Grab his leash," Rollie said.

CHAPTER NINE

Rollie was up before the girls and made breakfast. At the table, he told them he would be working, and that Gloria needed to stay with Mrs. Kravitz until he returned home.

Once the girls left for school, Rollie tidied up the kitchen and then walked over to see Mrs. Kravitz.

"If you could let Buddy out to the backyard around one that would be good," Rollie said.

"Will Gloria be coming over today?" Mrs. Kravitz said.

"Probably."

"I'll make some brownies," Mrs. Kravitz said.

After filling his travel mug with coffee, Rollie headed south to Rhode Island where Dennis Reiter disappeared from a nursing home.

The best route was 95 South and once he hooked up to it, it was a straight run to Providence, Rhode Island. His GPS gave a distance of 125 miles with a drive time of two hours.

At the age of eighty-one and confined to a wheelchair, it was highly unlikely that Reiter was responsible for any of the other missing persons on the list.

But everyone and everything needed to be cleared for Enache to collect his money.

After an hour, Rollie pulled into a highway rest stop to use the bathroom and fill his coffee mug.

It was a beautiful November morning, with bright sunshine and temperatures around sixty and Rollie sat at a picnic table for a bit.

Once he was back in the car, he drove straight through to Providence.

The GPS took Rollie right to the assisted living facility where Reiter had been a resident. The building was large, all on one floor and was blue with pink and grey trim.

He parked in the visitor's lot and entered the building through large and ornate front doors.

The massive lobby was designed to resemble a fine hotel. Plush carpeting, several sofas and chairs, two coffee tables and a full piano. Fresh cut flowers in vases adorned the tables and piano.

Rollie went to the reception desk where a woman wearing scrubs greeted him.

"May I help you?" she said.

Rollie showed her his identification.

"Are you really a private investigator?" she said.

"Cross my heart," Rollie said.

The woman smiled. "What can you possibly want here?" she said.

"I'd like to speak with whoever is in charge?" Rollie said.

"What about?"

"Dennis Reiter," Rollie said.

"Oh," the woman said.

•   •   •

Dorothy Wilson, administrator of the facility looked across her desk at Rollie. "Dennis Reiter was a true gentleman in every sense of the word," she said. "Always happy to talk to you and other residents. Always kind to the staff. He lost the use of his legs in an accident on a construction site, you know,"

"I know," Rollie said. "How long was he with you?"

"Three years," Wilson said. "He was living in a small home with caretakers on a daily basis. It got to be too much for him, and he applied and was accepted here. And I must tell you, he was quite happy here."

"What does it cost to be a resident here?" Rollie said.

"Seven thousand a month," Wilson said. "And Mr. Reiter could afford it and was quite happy to pay it."

"The day he disappeared, what can you tell me about it," Rollie said.

"Let me get Mr. Woods and we'll talk in the garden," Wilson said.

Woods was a tall, Black man of about fifty. He was a rugged-looking guy with a soft voice. He met Rollie and Wilson in the one-square-acre backyard gardens.

Fall mums were everywhere, but during summer months flower beds housed hundred of various flowers. Center in the garden was a large frog pond. Dozens of benches and tables allowed residents to sit and enjoy the garden during spring, summer and fall months. A flat stone path took you around the garden and to various tables and benches.

A six-foot-high wood fence surrounded the entire garden. A door in the fence was located close to the building on the left side.

"I took Mr. Reiter from his room to the gardens almost every day when the weather was nice," Woods said. "Sometimes he would have his lunch out here and if a ball game was on in the afternoon he would sit and listen to it on his radio."

"When was the last time you saw him?" Rollie said.

"That day he disappeared last August," Woods said. "I brought him out to the gardens right after lunch. The Yankees were playing a day game and he had his radio with him. I came back around three to check on him and he was gone, wheelchair and all."

"His radio?" Rollie said.

"No, actually," Woods said. "It was still playing. I remember it was the seventh inning."

"What did you do then?" Rollie said.

"First I checked the gardens, and then I checked his room," Woods said. "After that I got hold of Mrs. Wilson and we put out an emergency alert."

"Every room, hallway and closet were checked," Wilson said. "After that we called the police."

Rollie looked at the door in the fence. "What's on the other side of that door?"

Woods, Wilson, and Rollie walked to the door. The lock was a piece of cake to open with a credit card.

Woods opened the door. "Parking lot," he said. "And we checked it, the grounds and even the woods around the facility."

"Mrs. Wilson, would you remember the name of the detective who handled the case?" Rollie said.

"No, but I'm sure it's in the report," Wilson said.

•　　•　　•

Detective Pavano, a thirty-year veteran of the Providence Police department, handed Rollie a mug of coffee before he sat behind his desk.

"I remember Reiter because it was so strange the way he went missing," Pavano said. "A man who couldn't walk, you'd have to figure how far could he get? Not very far and yet we never found a trace of him."

"Did you check the lock on the door in the backyard gate?" Rollie said.

"No signs of forced entry," Pavano said.

"I could open that lock with a credit card," Rollie said.

"Sure, and do what, kidnap an old man in a wheelchair for his fortune?" Pavano said.

"Do you know why I was hired to investigate Dennis Reiter's disappearance?" Rollie said.

"You failed to mention that," Pavano said.

"He was on a short list to inherit north of $12,000,000," Rollie said.

Pavano stared at Rollie for a moment. "That changes the dynamics of things, doesn't it?" he said.

"How were his finances?" Rollie said.

Pavano stood, walked to a file cabinet, and returned with a folder and took his chair. He opened the folder. "Reiter was pretty well off due to a large settlement from a job-related accident," he said. "In addition, he collected $2,000 a month from social security. Expensive as that facility was, he could have lived there until he was ninety."

"Did he leave a will?" Rollie said.

Pavano flipped a page. "He left it all to the facility," he said.

"How much?"

"$300,000."

"Can I have the lawyer's name?" Rollie said.

· · ·

"Mr. Finch, I wasn't expecting to see you again so soon," Wilson said.

"An oversight on my part," Rollie said. "I was wondering if Mr. Reiter ever had any visitors."

"I'm not the person to ask," Wilson said.

"Do you keep logs on visitors?" Rollie said.

"Every visitor to see a guest gets signed in," Wilson said.

"What about workers, delivery people and others not here for residents?" Rollie said.

"Except for the mail, everybody logs in," Wilson said.

"I didn't log in. Twice," Rollie said.

"An oversight due to the nature of your visit, I'm sure," Wilson said. "I'll get you the logbook for last year. You can go through it in our lunchroom."

The cooks in the lunchroom made Rollie an excellent burger with fries and a milkshake.

He ate while he went through the logbook line-by-line. Rollie looked up when Woods approached the table with a tray of food. "Okay to join you?" he said.

"Please," Rollie said. "I was going to look for you anyway."

Woods looked at the logbook. "Let me guess, you're looking for visitors for Mr. Reiter."

"Know of any?" Rollie said.

"Not off hand," Woods said. "I would have seen him with a guest, but none come to mind."

"How long have you worked here?" Rollie said.

"Seventeen years."

"Seventeen years and you know for a fact Reiter didn't have one guest during the three years he resided here," Rollie said.

Woods smiled. "I'm here five days a week. I see it all," he said. "But sometimes I'd sit with Mr. Reiter in the garden or in the rec room during the winter and we'd talk. His number one complaint in life wasn't the loss of his legs. It was not having any family to visit him."

Rollie nodded. "Maybe so, but two days a week you weren't here," he said.

"I guess you have to be thorough," Woods said. "Let me get your card in case I think of anything."

After Woods finished his lunch, Rollie continued searching the logbook to the last page. He then took out his pen and signed the book.

Rollie returned the book and stopped by to tell Mrs. Wilson he was leaving.

"By the way, I was informed Reiter left everything he had to the facility," Rollie said.

"He did, but it's tied up in court, so we haven't received anything as yet," Wilson said.

"It's that way with missing person cases sometimes," Rollie said.

∙   ∙   ∙

In the middle of dinner, Giselle blurted out, "Dad, a boy at school asked if we could go to the movies together this weekend."

"Uh oh," Gloria said.

"Never you mind uh oh," Rollie said.

"Dad, your rule has always been sixteen for dating," Giselle said.

"I've heard it enough," Gloria said.

Rollie glared at Gloria. "I'll be quiet," she said.

"We worked it out, Dad," Grace said. "James and I are going to see the new Marvel movie on Saturday after work, so Giselle and her date can come along with us."

"I want to meet the boy first," Rollie said. "He comes to the house, agreed?"

"No problem, Dad," Giselle said.

"What's his name?" Rollie said.

"Alex Sale and he's a freshman like me," Giselle said.

"What time is the movie?" Rollie said.

"Seven o'clock," Giselle said.

"As long as he comes to the house first," Rollie said.

"I'll keep an eye on them, Dad," Grace said. "Don't worry."

"Who keeps an eye on you," Gloria said.

Rollie, Grace, and Giselle glared at Gloria.

"What?" Gloria said.

CHAPTER TEN

Reiter was an easy target. *Whoever kidnapped him knew where he would be at all times. Easy surveillance placed Reiter in the garden on a regular basis, especially on warm summer afternoons when he could listen to a ballgame on his radio.*

The door in the fence was no challenge at all to open. Waltz in, overpower Reiter, waltz out with his wheelchair and all and into a waiting car. Pick the right moment and it's sight unseen.

Rollie looked up from his notebook. Four of the six names proved to be no challenge at all for someone to kidnap and get rid of to make way for Enache to collect the $12,000,000.

He picked up the hard-line phone and called the airlines and reserved a flight to Charleston, South Carolina for Sunday morning, returning Monday evening.

He found the girls watching TV in the living room. "Girls, a moment please," he said. "I have to go to South Carolina Sunday morning, returning Monday night. Grace, I know you are responsible enough to watch your sisters on Sunday, but Monday please make sure Gloria stays with Mrs. Kravitz until I get home."

"Sure, Dad," Grace said. "No problem."

Rollie looked at Gloria. "And no arguments from you," he said. "You do as your sister tells you."

"Which sister?" Gloria said.

"Why is the youngest always the hardest?" Rollie said. "I'll be in my office."

Using his cell phone, Rollie called Joanna.

"Rollie, I was just thinking about you and the girls," she said.

"How far away are you from Charleston?" Rollie said.

"The old cliche—a hop, skip and a jump comes to mind," Joanna said. "Why?"

"I thought I could take you to dinner Sunday night," Rollie said.

"What are you talking about?" Joanna said.

"I have to be in Charlestown Sunday on business," Rollie said. "I thought I'd take you to dinner afterward."

"No," Joanna said.

"No?"

"I'll cook for you Sunday night," Joanna said. "At my house."

"It won't be until around seven," Rollie said.

"Not a problem," Joanna said.

"I'll call you when I get there," Rollie said.

"You'd better," Joanna said.

After hanging up with Joanna, Rollie typed his notes into the document on his computer.

In his mind, there was little doubt that someone targeted the missing six to eliminate them from collecting the tontine money.

As a homicide detective, the obvious suspect was Enache.

Rollie took out his pen and jotted down some thoughts.

Would an eighty-six-year-old man have the wherewithal, the strength, guile and endurance to enact the deaths of six people?

Not without help.

The other thing was all six were related either through blood or marriage. Most men, except for the truly psychotic, stop just short of killing their relatives.

If all 100 members of the tontine were either dead or missing, who did

Enache have close enough in his life that would commit murder for him?
A hired hit man?
Someone who would get a cut of the $12,000,000.

Rollie typed his notes into the document on his computer and called it a day.

The girls were watching the ending of some movie on television.

"Gloria, as soon as that movie is over, we'll take Buddy for his walk," Rollie said. "Grace, Giselle, get ready for bed."

Five minutes later, Rollie and Gloria were taking Buddy for a walk around the block.

"Dad, Giselle said you'll be teaching her to drive soon," Gloria said.

"As soon as she gets her learner's permit," Rollie said.

"Am I a runt?" Gloria said.

"What?"

"A runt. That's what they call me," Gloria said.

"Your sisters?"

"Who else?"

"Want me to speak to them?" Rollie said.

"No. I can handle it," Gloria said. "It's just, Grace is five-seven and Giselle is almost as tall and I'm only five-one."

"Grace is also four years older than you," Rollie said.

"I know," Gloria said.

When they circled the block and reached home, Rollie said, "I want to show you something."

They entered the house, removed the leash, and went to Rollie's bedroom. "See those faint pencil marks on the door frame?" Rollie said. "Your mother made those."

"I never noticed them before," Gloria said.

"That last line there is the last one she made," Rollie said. "That's Grace at your age. Can you read it?"

"Sixty-one inches," Gloria said.

"Five-one," Rollie said.

Gloria smiled at Rollie. "Good night, Dad," she said.

After Gloria went to her room, Rollie returned to his office for a few minutes. He opened the document on his computer and read his notes. He reserved judgment until after he investigated the remaining two on the list, but even a civilian could see they were eliminated for the money.

The question was, who was doing the eliminating?

CHAPTER ELEVEN

"I see your point, Mr. Finch," Rose said as he read through Rollie's reports.

Seated opposite Rose's desk, Rollie sipped coffee from the cup Rose offered him and nodded. "If the last two names prove anything like the first six, someone was overlooked," Rollie said. "Or Enache is behind it all."

"Which would be ridiculous to imagine," Rose said.

"Which, in turn puts Enache in grave danger," Rollie said. "If he isn't responsible for the missing six."

"I see your point," Rose said. "But my responsibility is to release the funds to the last person alive in the tontine. Anything else is peripheral to my duty."

"Not if murder is involved," Rollie said. "Murder changes things dramatically."

Rose nodded. "I agree but let me ask you this. You were hired to investigate the six unaccounted for members of the tontine, not get involved in murder. Once you have done your job, if murder is the cause of the missing six members, isn't that a job for the police?"

"If it can be proven and if there is enough evidence to proceed and if Enache is still alive after he collects his money and if anybody still cares about a sixty-year-old tontine," Rollie said.

"That's a lot of ifs," Rose said.

"After I finish the last two names, I'll talk to my contacts at the PD," Rollie said. "And when can I meet with Enache?"

"I can arrange that anytime you'd like," Rose said.

"As soon as I finish the last two names," Rollie said.

Rose nodded. "Once you have proven all six are truly missing, I can only stall for so long before I am forced to release the funds to Enache. Thirty days in fact."

"A lot can happen in thirty days," Rollie said.

•   •   •

Stopping by Rose's office was one of two reasons Rollie went to Manhattan. The second reason was a meeting with Police Commissioner Andrews.

Andrews received Rollie in his office at One Police Plaza.

"I have to admit I was disappointed when you turned down the position of Assistant Chief of Detectives, but I reviewed your recommendation carefully and I have to agree with you," Andrews said.

"Have you told him yet?" Rollie said.

"He's on his way down right now," Andrews said.

"Then I better take off," Rollie said. "I don't want him to think he's second choice."

"I understand," Andrews said.

•   •   •

"I admit on the surface it sounds like a criminal matter, but without proof there is very little you can do about it," Gitter said.

"Besides, weren't you hired just to investigate the missing six members?" Schram asked.

"Yes, but it's obvious what's happened," Rollie said.

"So, what do you plan to do?" Gitter said.

"Finish the remaining two and make a decision then," Rollie said. "But the other reason I'm here is to find out about the other matter you mentioned when we met with Rose."

"Robert Marks," Gitter said.

"The real estate developer, the one accused of killing his wife?" Rollie said.

"The grand jury convenes in late January," Schram said. "We'd like you to take a look at the evidence and tell us what you see."

"You think he's innocent?" Rollie said.

"We're defending him," Gitter said.

"I'll take a look," Rollie said.

"Let us know what you think, and we'll go from there," Schram said.

"I'll get back to you on the tontine investigation after I've finished with the list," Rollie said.

"We'll be interested to hear the results," Schram said.

•　　•　　•

Thirty days after he documents the missing six are truly out of the picture, Enache gets the $12,000,000. Rollie didn't believe in coincidence. Someone unknown at this time was systematically removing the surviving members to allow Enache to claim the prize.

But who?

Rollie thought about it as he drove home along Queens Boulevard.

Rose, Gitter and Schram were correct when they said he only signed on to validate the missing six were truly missing.

But he could not turn his back on murder. The homicide detective in him wouldn't allow it.

He parked in the driveway, was about to go next door to Mrs. Kravitz when he heard Buddy barking inside. Rollie opened the door and was greeted by Buddy, who followed him to the living room.

Where he found Mrs. Kravitz and Gloria playing a video game on the television.

"Take that, you little scamp," Mrs. Kravitz said.

"Dad, she's beating the pants off me," Gloria said. "Gloria, I'm sure Mrs. Kravitz has better things to do besides play video games," Rollie said.

"Actually, Gloria, let's take Buddy for a walk around the block," Mrs. Kravitz said.

"I'll get the leash," Gloria said.

"Well, okay then," Rollie said and went to his office.

He set the briefcase on his desk and then went to the kitchen to make some coffee. When he returned to his desk, the hard-line phone rang.

"Rollie, it's Bill," Teal said.

"How are things in Midtown South?" Rollie said.

"A funny thing," Teal said. "I was summoned to the commissioner's office today."

"Oh?" Rollie said.

"The commissioner, chief of police and chief of detectives was there," Teal said.

"Really?"

"Cut the bullshit," Teal said. "They offered me the position you turned down."

"Assistant Chief of Detectives?" Rollie said.

"No, chief cook and bottle washer," Teal said.

"Congratulations, Bill. You deserve it," Rollie said.

"I don't know if I deserve it, but I'm certainly going to take it," Teal said.

"I'll pop over and buy you lunch tomorrow," Rollie said.

"And I will let you," Teal said.

"See you around twelve thirty," Rollie said.

Rollie hung up and went to the kitchen and poked around the refrigerator. A bit later, Gloria and Buddy returned.

"Do hour homework?" Rollie said.

"At Mrs. Kravitz's before we came over," Gloria said.

"We need to go grocery shopping," Rollie said.

"I already made a list," Gloria said.

CHAPTER TWELVE

Teal bit into a double bacon-cheeseburger and then wiped juice off his chin. "I haven't had any real food since we last went to lunch," he said. "I don't care how much slop you put on tofu, it's not the real thing."

"But you passed your physical?" Rollie said.

"By the skin of my teeth, but yeah."

"When do you report to your new job?" Rollie said.

"Thirty days or as soon as they find a replacement," Teal said.

"Have you told your wife?"

"Not yet. I'll do it when I get home or else, she'll be figuring out ways to spend my raise."

"So, you won't mind another teaming up with me for another investigation?" Rollie said.

"If by teaming up you mean you do all the work and I take all the credit, what are you offering?" Teal said.

"Something I signed on to do which might turn out to be something else entirely," Rollie said. "I need another week or so before I'm certain."

"When you're certain, let me know if it's something I can jump on board with," Teal said. "In the meantime, let's order some dessert."

•   •   •

The girls were in the kitchen when Rollie returned home. He took a can of ginger ale to his office, sat at his desk, and opened the file on Robert Marks that Gitter and Schram asked him to take a look at.

Robert Marks was a self-made man. A product of Hell's Kitchen, born fifty-three years ago to an unwed mother, he scraped and fought his way through high school and city college and after a three-year stint in the Army, returned to New York to work in real estate.

Thirty years later, Marks was worth nearly five billion and amassed a real estate empire that spanned coast-to-coast and globally.

He built everything from luxury high-rise buildings to golf courses to casinos and everything in between.

A genius at his profession, Marks was the opposite in his private life. Married four times and each marriage was a disaster. The first three ended in divorce, the fourth in murder, of which Marks was accused.

Married to his fourth wife Justine just three years, the first year was good, the final two, by Marks's own account were a war zone. Justine was just thirty and Marks wanted several more children to go along with the five he already had.

Justine wanted money and expensive things and the marriage soon evolved into the hot zone.

Three months ago, Justine was stabbed multiple times in the living room of the penthouse apartment at Marks Tower on Fifth Avenue. According to Marks, he came home and found his wife dead on the floor.

Responding police to Marks's 911 call found blood on Mark's right knee, his right hand, and his fingerprints on the hunting knife that killed Justine.

Marks posted his $10,000,000 bail, surrendered his passport and hired Gitter and Schram to defend him.

Rollie closed the file, went to his bedroom to change into sweats and then did thirty minutes on the step-climber and another thirty minutes on the Bowflex. For once he concentrated on the workout and not the case at hand.

Afterward, Rollie took a quick shower and tossed on a warm-up suit and went to the kitchen to help the girls prepare dinner.

"We got this, Dad," Grace said. "Go relax and we'll call you when it's ready."

Rollie returned to his office and sat at his desk.

He picked up the file on Tamas Lupu. A forty-year veteran of the fire department, an Army veteran as well, Lupu disappeared from his retirement home on Shore Island off the coast of South Carolina.

Lupu was eighty-four years old when he went missing.

Rollie closed the file and went to the table when Grace called him.

"Dad, I got my learner's permit," Giselle announced as he took his chair.

CHAPTER THIRTEEN

Rollie and Gloria were watching a movie in the living room when James Seymour, Grace's date and classmate from school arrived.

As he rang the doorbell, Gloria said, "Stupid is here."

"Let him in," Rollie said. "And don't call him stupid."

Gloria went to and opened the door.

"It's me, James and I'm here to take Grace to the movies," James said.

"Oh God," Gloria said.

Rollie greeted James in the living room. "Hello, James," Rollie said.

"Hello, sir," James said. "I'm here to take Grace to the movies."

"I thought you were here to mow the lawn," Gloria said.

"The lawn? It's November, but if you want me to, I can do it tomorrow," James said.

"Oh God," Gloria said. "Nobody is this…"

"That's enough out of you," Rollie said. "Go tell Grace that James is here."

Gloria went to Grace's room.

"Have a seat, James," Rollie said.

"Thank you, sir," James said and continued to stand.

Rollie took his chair and looked at James. "James?" Rollie said.

"Yes sir?"

"Never mind," Rollie said.

Grace returned and said, "She said to keep him occupied so she can make an entrance," she said. "So, we can play fetch."

"Fetch?" James said.

The doorbell rang again, and Gloria dashed to the door and opened it.

"Hi… umm, does Giselle Finch live here?" a boy of sixteen said.

"No, and you have pimples," Gloria said.

"What? No, see, I'm Alex Sale and I'm here to take her to the movies," Alex said.

"Oh God," Gloria said. "Another one."

Rollie appeared at the door. "Come in, Alex. I'm Gloria's father," he said.

"I'm Alex Sale, sir and I'm here to take Giselle to the movies."

"Come in and have a seat next to James," Rollie said.

"But James is standing, sir," Alex said.

"So he is," Rollie said. "Gloria, tell Giselle her date is here."

Gloria dashed off to Giselle's room and returned a moment later. "She said to keep him occupied," Gloria said. "I could get a ball and we…"

"That's more than enough out of you," Rollie said.

Grace, followed by Giselle, made their entrance. "Scarlet and Melanie are here," Gloria said.

"Who's Scarlet?" James said.

"Never mind," Grace said, glaring at Gloria.

"What time does the movie end?" Rollie said.

"Nine forty-five," Grace said.

"Boys, I expect you to have my daughters home by eleven," Rollie said.

"We will, sir," James said.

"Alright, have a good time," Rollie said. "Grace, drive carefully."

"I will, Dad. Don't worry," Grace said.

As they walked to the door, Alex said, "Who's Melanie?"

Gloria went to the window. "It's dumb and dumber meet Bill and Ted," she said.

"Go change," Rollie said. "I'm taking my youngest to dinner."

"Remind me not to date until I'm thirty," Gloria said.

CHAPTER FOURTEEN

Rollie's plane took off at 8:15 in the morning and landed in Charlestown at 9:50.

He packed just an overnight bag that fit in the overhead compartment, so he zipped right out to the terminal, bypassing luggage pickup.

Before picking up his rental car, he called Joanna on his cell phone.

"I'm in Charlestown," Rollie said.

"Had breakfast?" Joanna said.

"At the airport."

"Where are you off to?"

"Shore Island."

"That's about an hour south."

"I'll find it with the GPS."

"Skip lunch and bring your appetite," Joanna said.

"I should be there at seven," Rollie said.

"Have fun at whatever it is you're doing," Joanna said.

Next, Rollie called home. Grace answered the call.

"Hi, Dad."

"I'm in South Carolina," Rollie said. "What are you guys going to do today?"

"Maybe the dog park, if it's nice."

"Alright but keep your cell phone on so I can call you later," Rollie said.

"Of course," Grace said.

"I'll talk to you later," Rollie said. "Have fun."

After hanging up, Rollie rented a car with a GPS and headed for Shore Island. The drive, as Joanna said, took about an hour. A half-mile long bridge connected the island to mainland South Carolina.

About seventy-five square miles, Shore Island is home to 40,000 residents and hundreds of thousands of tourists during season. With twenty miles of pristine beaches and dozens of beachfront hotels, Shore Island is a major tourist destination for those who love golf and beaches.

Lupu's retirement home overlooked the beach and fit right in with the major hotels. Bright blue with a pink stucco roof, the retirement home housed three hundred residents. Constructed in a horseshoe shape, the building was hurricane proof with enough generators to power through major storms, so said the brochure Rollie read in the lobby as he waited for the facility manager.

Paul Watson, a man in his sixties, tall and thin, was the facility director and he met Rollie in the ornate lobby.

"Mr. Finch, my receptionist tells me you are a private investigator interested in Mr. Lupu," Watson said.

Three hours later, after a tour of the facility and the gardens and grounds, Rollie still had no answer as to how Lupu disappeared.

Lupu was eighty-four at the time he vanished, but he was a bull of a man, healthy and strong who exercised daily.

"This is not a nursing home, it's a retirement community," Watson said several times. "Our residents are free to come and go as they please. Oh we have two nurses on call at all times and a well-trained staff to assist them, but for the most part our residents are free to do as they please as if they were in their own homes."

"Which was Lupu's apartment?" Rollie said.

"Number one-thirty-one, but it's occupied," Watson said.

"I just want to see where it is," Rollie said.

Watson led Rollie down a long hallway where each door was numbered.

"Here we go, one-thirty-one," Watson said.

Rollie looked up and down the hallway. It would be difficult to kidnap a man from his apartment and not be seen doing it.

"What were his habits?" Rollie said.

"Habits?"

"What did he like to do?" Rollie said.

"Why, I have no idea?"

"Who does?"

.   .   .

"Most mornings you could find Tamas in the gym before eight o'clock," a caretaker said. "He was very fit and healthy for his age. Most evenings you could find him in a lawn chair at the beach, watching the sunset. He used to say it reminded him of his wife."

Rollie and the caretaker were in the lobby and Rollie looked through the glass doors at the beach across the street.

"He'd walk there?" Rollie said.

"Of course," the caretaker. "He had the fitness level of a fifty-year-old."

"Why did he live here?" Rollie said.

"Judging from the way he talked about his wife and from the way he decorated his apartment with her photos, I'd say he was lonely and wanted to be around people."

"And he'd sit alone on the beach and watch the sunset?"

"Almost every night," the caretaker said. "He told me watching the sunset was his wife's favorite thing to do."

"Can you take me to Mr. Watson's office, please?" Rollie said.

．　　．　　．

Can you show me the police report so I can speak to the investigating detective?" Rollie said.

Watson opened a drawer in his desk and produced a police report. Rollie scanned it and wrote the name of the detective in his notebook.

"What is this about if I may ask?" Watson said.

"If he had lived, Mr. Lupu was on a very short list to inherit $12,000,00," Rollie said.

"Why… I'm speechless," Watson said.

"So is Mr. Lupu," Rollie said.

．　　．　　．

Shore Island fell under the authority of the County sheriff's department and Detective Sherman Whitt was the investigating officer.

"The way it went down," Whitt said in his southern drawl. "Is when Mr. Lupu didn't return to the complex by ten o'clock, one of the staff went to the beach to look for him. What they found was his folding chair on the sand and no Mr. Lupu."

"Is it possible he went into the water?" Rollie said.

"Unlikely," Whitt said. "His chair was thirty feet back at low tide, but the Coast Guard did a search and found nothing."

"From what I was told, he missed his wife terribly," Rollie said.

"If you're thinking suicide, how many wait nine years after their wife died to do it?" Whitt said. "And there was no note, no nothing."

"How were his finances?" Rollie said.

"His pension was $63,000 a year plus benefits," Whitt said. "Another $24,000 a year from social security. $150,000 in a savings account and $12,000 in checking."

"Who did he leave it to?" Rollie said.

"Nobody," Whitt said. "He and his wife never had children. We searched for family but found none. It's still with the courts."

"Thanks for your time," Rollie said.

"Wait," Whitt said. "Why the interest in an old missing person's case from a New York City detective?"

"Mr. Lupu, had he lived stood a very good chance at inheriting twelve million dollars," Rollie said.

"That changes things," Whitt said. "Maybe I'll take another look at this."

"Let me know if you find anything," Rollie said.

•　　•　　•

Rollie drove back to the retirement complex, parked, picked up a container of coffee and a small coffee shot on the street and then walked to the beach.

It was five in the afternoon and already getting dark. He sipped coffee and watched the road behind him. Traffic on the road was non-existent. Lupu vanished in early May when it still got dark before seven.

Lupu sat in his chair, watched the sunset and shortly after dark, a car drove up and snatched him off the beach.

Even though he was healthy and strong, how much of a problem would it have been to overpower an eighty-four-year-old man?

As with the others, surveillance was necessary to learn Lupu's habits.

Once they learned where and when Lupu would be, it was an easy task to apprehend him.

Rollie used his cell phone to call home.

"Hi, Dad," Grace said.

"What are you guys up to?" Rollie said.

"Making dinner. We took Buddy to the dog park," Grace said.

"I'll call later around nine," Rollie said.

"Okay, Dad," Grace said.

Rollie pocketed his phone and kept watching the road. Since he arrived, not one car had passed.

"Easy pickings," Rollie said aloud.

He returned to his car and headed for Joanna's house.

CHAPTER FIFTEEN

When she opened the door for Rollie, Joanna smiled broadly and then gave him a warm hug. She wore white slacks, yellow top, and white socks without shoes. She stood five-foot nine-inches tall and rarely wore high-heels because she was a bit self-conscious of her height.

"I like your house," Rollie said.

"It's small, but perfect for one," Joanna said. "Come to the living room, I just made fresh coffee."

Rollie took a seat on the sofa while Joanna went to the kitchen. She returned with two mugs of coffee and set them on the coffee table.

"It's okay to remove the jacket and tie, Rollie," Joanna said. "You're off duty."

Rollie stood up to remove his tie and jacket and then sat beside Joanna.

"The girls okay?" Joanna said.

"Fine. You're mother okay?"

"Fine," Joanna said.

Rollie took a sip of coffee. Joanna took a sip of coffee. They looked at each other.

"Why is this so awkward?" Joanna said.

"Speaking for just myself, I haven't been with a woman since my wife died more than four years ago," Rollie said.

Joanna nodded. "And since my divorce I've practically lived like a nun," she said.

"Hence the awkwardness," Rollie said.

"Hence," Joanna said. "So, I have a suggestion. Before we have dinner, let us go into my bedroom and find out if our rusty equipment still works."

"Suggest?" Rollie said.

"More like a request."

Joanna stood up and extended her right hand. Rollie took it and stood.

"Why do you look like you're on your way to your own execution?" Joanna said.

"It's been a long time," Rollie said.

"Me, too. So, it's about time," Joanna said.

•   •   •

"That was clumsy, awkward, comical and funny," Joanna said.

"Don't sugarcoat it," Rollie said.

"And the best thing to happen to me in a decade," Joanna said. "Can you do it again?"

"Maybe if you feed me," Rollie said.

Joanna burst out laughing. "Dinner is keeping warm," she said.

•   •   •

Over dessert, Rollie called home.

"Hey, Dad," Grace said.

"Everything okay?" Rollie said.

"Sure," Grace said. "I'll have Giselle and the squirt in bed by ten.

What time will you be home tomorrow?"

"Around five."

"I'll make sure Gloria is with Mrs. Kravitz," Grace said.

"Okay, see you tomorrow," Rollie said.

After he hung up, Joanna topped off their coffee cups. "Got your strength back?" she said.

Rollie sipped from his cup. "Let's find out," he said.

Joanna stood up from the table. "Let's," she said.

. . .

"I thought my brain was going to explode," Joanna said as she rested her head on Rollie's chest. "You are much stronger than I thought."

"Did I hurt you?" Rollie said.

"No, but I can see how you surprise the bad guys," Joanna said. "They underestimate you."

Rollie ran his fingers through her hair.

"Isn't that why you're here, to catch bad guys?" Joanna said.

"In a sense," Rollie said. "It's a missing person's case, actually."

"When I come for Thanksgiving, you'll sleep on that daybed, won't you?" Joanna said.

"Afraid so," Rollie said. "But my door is open to after hours visits."

"What time does your plane leave tomorrow?"

"Two."

"I have to be at school by eight fifteen."

"Not a problem, I have work to do before the flight," Rollie said.

"I'm sleepy."

"Me, too."

Joanna reached across Rollie and turned off the bedside lamp.

. . .

In the morning, Rollie and Joanna made love before taking a shower. Joanna dressed casually in a skirt and blouse, while Rollie wore his suit with a clean shirt.

They had a light breakfast at the table, consisting of toast with jam and coffee.

"Now that you got your mojo back, don't go Tom catting around on me," Joanna said.

"No worries," Rollie said. "My girls keep me too busy."

"See you in two weeks," Joanna said.

"You bet," Rollie said.

After they parted, Rollie drove back to Shore Island and found Paul Watson in his office.

"Mr. Finch, I wasn't expecting you back," Watson said.

"I know, but I wanted to follow up with you," Rollie said.

"I have staff meetings today, so could you make it quick," Watson said.

"Actually, I'd like to attend a staff meeting," Rollie said.

"That's out of the question," Watson said.

"The status of this has escalated from missing person to murder," Rollie said.

"Murder?"

"I'll try to keep the name of your complex out of it, but I need to address your staff," Rollie said.

"Follow me to the conference room," Watson said.

About forty people were in the conference room. Nurses, administrative staff, maintenance people, cooks and gardeners and caretakers sat at a large conference table in the boardroom. Bagels, donuts, and coffee were available to all.

Watson introduced Rollie and told the group why he was there.

"I'll be as brief as possible," Rollie said. "Some of you saw me yesterday. I'm a private detective from New York City and I've been hired by a law firm to investigate the disappearance of Tamas Lupu. Is there anybody here who isn't familiar with Mr. Lupu, raise your hand."

Nobody raised their hands.

"It was recorded that Mr. Lupu was a missing person's case, but I have reason to believe he was murdered," Rollie said.

After the slight buzz from the crowd died down, Rollie said, "How many of you saw Mr. Lupu leave with his folding chair to sit on the beach, raise your hands."

Half the group held up their hands.

"So here is the question rolling around in my mind," Rollie said. "If Mr. Lupu left around seven to watch the sunset, why wasn't he missed until ten p.m. that night? Three hours is a long time not to be missed. Can anybody explain that to me?"

No one spoke or even moved.

"Okay, let's try this," Rollie said. "How was it someone finally noticed Mr. Lupu didn't return?"

A woman raised her hand.

"Yes?" Rollie said.

"I work in the laundry," she said. "We do laundry and dry cleaning for residents who want it. I was leaving for the night at ten and noticed his chair still on the beach."

"In the dark?" Rollie said.

"It was a bright moon, and I could see what I thought was a chair. I went to investigate, and it was Mr. Lupu's chair," the woman said. "I went back in and alerted security."

"And?" Rollie said.

A uniformed security guard raised his hand. "We did a thorough search of the facility and then called the police," he said.

"The police might be back now that they think murder instead of missing person," Rollie said.

• • •

Detective Sherman Whitt handed Rollie a cup of coffee as Rollie took a chair in front of the detective's desk.

"This morning I pulled all the paperwork of Mr. Lupu and met with my superior," Whitt said. "He agrees I should take a look at the murder angle."

"Give me a call at my New York office," Rollie said. "We can exchange information."

"I will," Whitt said.

CHAPTER SIXTEEN

Rollie picked Gloria up at Mrs. Kravitz's house and they took Buddy for a walk around the block.

"How is Joanna?" Gloria said.

"She's fine and looking forward to Thanksgiving," Rollie said.

"We're looking forward to seeing her," too, Gloria said.

"I've been thinking about something for when she's here," Rollie said. "We'll put it to a vote tonight."

They reached home. "We should start dinner for the working girls," Gloria said.

"We should," Rollie said.

Grace and Giselle came home to a dinner of baked chicken breasts and mashed potatoes with corn and carrots.

"Okay, girls, I'd like to put this to a vote," Rollie said. "When Joanna is here, I'd like to take her to see the Christmas tree lighting at Rock Center on Friday. In favor, raise your hands."

The girls held up their hands.

"Can we also see the windows at Macy's and Saks?" Grace said.

"We can see all of them," Rollie said. "Right now, I'd like to see you and Giselle do your homework."

"I got the dishes," Gloria said.

Rollie took a cup of coffee to his office, sat behind his desk, and called Joanna.

"As odd as this may sound, I was about to dial your number," Joanna said.

"We had a family meeting at dinner and agreed on some surprises for you on Thanksgiving," Rollie said.

"I love surprises," Joanna said. "In fact, I loved the surprise you gave me this morning."

"Next week I have to go to Florida for this investigation," Rollie said. "Feel adventurous?"

"I can't go to Florida, I have school," Joanna said.

"The old cliché hop skip and a jump comes to mind," Rollie said. "South Carolina is maybe ninety minutes by plane to Florida. You can be my assistant for the day."

"God, Rollie, you're tempting me," Joanna said.

"I'll call you back tomorrow with details," Rollie said.

"Should I do this?"

"You should," Rollie said.

Joanna sighed. "Okay, but we better be going someplace nice," she said.

After chatting for a bit with Joanna, Rollie got to work writing a report on Lupu. There was no doubt in his mind that Lupu, and the others were kidnapped and murdered for the tontine payoff.

The question remained, who was doing the killing?

After writing his report on paper, Rollie typed it into a document in his computer.

Then he went to the kitchen where Grace and Giselle were finishing their homework.

Gloria was in the living room with Buddy, watching television.

"Grab your jacket and the leash, we'll take Buddy for a walk," Rollie said.

They took Buddy around the block and when they returned home, Grace and Giselle were done with their homework.

"I have to go into Manhattan tomorrow morning," Rollie said. "I should be home by no later than four."

"Okay, Dad," Grace said.

.　　●　　.

Rollie was a light sleeper, and he woke up around two in the morning when he heard Buddy at the kitchen sliding doors.

"What is it, boy?" Rollie said when he went to the kitchen.

Buddy pawed the glass doors.

"Need to go out?" Rollie said.

He unlocked the door and slid it open and Buddy raced into the yard and disappeared behind the lone tree in the yard.

"Now what is he up to?" Rollie said.

Rollie flicked on the outside floodlight and walked to the tree. Buddy was sitting beside an orange and white tabby cat who was in the process of giving birth. Two kittens were already out and a third was on the way.

Wearing a robe and slippers, Grace emerged from the house and said, "Dad, what's going on?"

It looks like Buddy is about to become an uncle," Rollie said.

Giselle, also wearing a robe and slippers showed up and said," What's wrong, is something wrong?"

"Buddy is about to become an uncle," Grace said.

"What?" Gloria said.

"That's three," Rollie said.

"Why is everybody in the backyard?" Gloria said as she tied the belt on her robe.

"Buddy is an uncle," Giselle said.

"What?" Gloria said.

"Dad, it's freezing out here," Grace said.

"Girls, go to where we keep cardboard boxes in the garage, get a good sized one, put some towels on the bottom," Rollie said.

The girls were gone for five minutes and when they returned, Rollie said," We're up to four now."

"Dad, what do we do?" Gloria said.

Rollie took the box to the cat and set it beside her. "No one is going to hurt you," he said.

While Buddy watched with keen interest, Rollie placed the cat and four kittens inside the box and picked it up.

"We'll take her to my office, so she has some privacy," Rollie said.

Rollie carried the box into the house, followed by the girls and Buddy. In his office, Rollie set the box down in the rear of the office beside the wall.

"It's freezing in here, too, Dad," Grace said.

Rollie adjusted the thermostat on the wall to heat the garage.

"Well, she has four," Gloria said. "How many do you think she'll have?"

"We'll find out in the morning," Rollie said. "Everybody back to bed."

Buddy got down beside the box.

"I think Buddy is staying put for the night," Rollie said.

CHAPTER SEVENTEEN

Rollie, armed with a mug of coffee, entered his office, and looked at Buddy who was still beside the cardboard box.

"Long night, huh," Rollie said.

Buddy sat up as Rollie looked into the box.

The girls came up beside him.

"Six," Gloria said.

"Gloria, get Buddy's leash and we'll take him for a walk," Rollie said. "Grace, you and Giselle get breakfast started. You don't want to be late for school."

Thirty minutes later, at the breakfast table, Gloria said, "Dad, what are we supposed to do with a box full of kittens?"

"Grace, don't they do adoptions at your pet store?" Rollie said.

Grace smiled. "They do," she said.

"We'll talk to Mr. Fudderman after school," Giselle said.

"Speaking of school," Rollie said.

Grace stood up. "Come on squirt, let's go," she said.

After the girls left for school, Rollie shaved, took a shower, and dressed in slacks, a pullover shirt, and carried a cup of coffee to the garage.

Buddy was beside the cardboard box. Rollie stood over the box and watched the kittens nurse.

"Hold down the fort, Buddy," Rollie said.

Rollie drove to the large pet store where Grace and Giselle

worked after school and purchased a bed for the cat and her kittens, a litter box, litter, food and water bowls and a bag of cat food.

He drove home, set everything up and under the watchful eye of Buddy; Rollie transferred cat and kittens to the comfortable bed.

"Come on, Buddy, I'll take you for a walk around the block before I go," Rollie said.

. . .

Rose scanned the printed report on Lupu that Rollie handed him and said, "I must admit, Mr. Finch, you are quite good and very thorough."

"I'll be going to Florida this Friday for Mr. Wendt," Rollie said.

Rose nodded as he set the document on his desk. "Do you need additional expense money?" he said.

"No," Rollie said. "I'll probably be bringing you receipts."

"When will you be back?" Rose said.

"Sunday night. I'll report back to you on Monday," Rollie said.

"I should be able to close the book on this within forty-five days or so," Rose said.

"I'm just curious about something," Rollie said. "What happens to the money if Mr. Enache dies before he collects?"

"There is a clause in the tontine that if no one survives to collect the money it all goes to charity," Rose said.

"Who oversees that?" Rollie said.

"Originally it was my father's duty," Rose said. "It's been passed down to me."

"Let's hope Enache lives long enough to collect so you can be done with it," Rollie said.

. . .

"Not that I don't appreciate an unexpected free lunch," Teal said. "But what's the cost?"

"Who said there's a cost?" Rollie said.

"My cop instinct and twenty-six years of knowing you," Teal said. "That's who said."

"A bit harsh," Rollie said.

"Never mind harsh," Teal said. "What is the cost of this double bacon-cheeseburger?"

"This case I'm working on, I may call on you down the road," Rollie said.

"Tell me about it," Teal said.

"Next week when I get back," Rollie said.

"Where are you going?"

"Key Largo on Friday."

"The Bogie and Bacall Key Largo?"

"That's the one," Rollie said.

"And this is part of what you're working on?" Teal said.

"It is."

"So, you're being paid to fly to Key Largo and bask in sunshine for the weekend," Teal said.

"About it."

"And you want my help?"

"Down the road," Rollie said. "And as you're the new Assistant Chief of Detectives, you're in a position to give it."

"What have I done wrong?" Teal said.

• • •

The girls were doing homework in the kitchen when Rollie returned home.

"Mr. Fudderman is coming over in about an hour to look at the kittens," Grace said. "The store does a lot of adoptions every year."

"We see you bought a lot of stuff for them," Giselle said.

"This morning," Rollie said. "Where's Buddy?"

"With his girlfriend," Gloria said.

Rollie grabbed a can of ginger ale from the fridge and went to his office. Buddy was asleep beside the cat bed. Mama cat was also asleep with her litter of kittens curled into tiny balls at her stomach.

Buddy looked up at Rollie and then went back to sleep.

Rollie sat at his desk and used his computer to check airline flights and hotels in Key Largo.

Then he called Joanna.

"Rollie, I was just thinking of calling you," Joanna said.

"There's a flight that gets me to Charlestown at six forty-five Friday night," Rollie said. "And a connecting flight that arrives in Miami at ten fifteen. I can meet you in Charleston at the gate."

"Should I do this, Rollie?" Joanna said.

"Give me one good reason why not?" Rollie said.

"What time is that flight?" Joanna said.

"I'll book it and call you back," Rollie said.

Before he called the airlines, Grace entered the office. "Dad, Mr. Fudderman is here to see the kittens."

"Bring him in," Rollie said.

Mr. Fudderman, a tall, balding man in his fifties was escorted in by the girls. He shook hands with Rollie. "Your daughters are wonderful workers," he said.

"They get it from their mother," Rollie said.

"The kittens are over here," Gloria said.

Everyone walked to the rear of the office where mama cat and kittens were being guarded by Buddy.

Fudderman knelt in front of the cat bed and picked up at kitten and Buddy whined. Gloria patted Buddy and said, "It's okay, boy, no one is going to hurt them."

"When they turn twelve weeks, we'll have them checked out by our vet and if all are healthy, we can put them up for adoption at the store," Fudderman said. "You girls can make it your project to see they get good homes."

"We will," Grace said.

"Mr. Finch, didn't I see you in the store earlier today?" Fudderman said.

"The cat needed a few things," Rollie said.

"I have to be getting back to the store now," Fudderman said.

"We'll walk you out," Grace said.

Gloria stayed behind. "Dad, what do we do with the cat after the kittens are gone?" she said.

"Ask Buddy," Rollie said.

Gloria looked at Buddy, who was licking mama cat's face. "I think I'll help Grace and Giselle start dinner," she said.

After Gloria left the office, Rollie called the airlines and booked a flight to Charleston and two flights to Miami. Then he called Joanna.

"Flight 1145, gate 23," Rollie said.

"I've never done something this impetuous," Joanna said.

"Then it's about time," Rollie said.

CHAPTER EIGHTEEN

For the next several days, Rollie studied his notes and made a chart on the locations, dates and times of the first five victim's disappearances.

He was convinced all five had been murdered by the same person. The motive was the $12,000,000.

The benefactor was Enache, an eighty-six-year-old man.

The big question was who was pulling the strings?

An eighty-six-year-old man or someone waiting in the wings for the money.

At breakfast, on Friday morning, Rollie gave the girls the number to the hotel he reserved. "Mind Mrs. Kravitz this afternoon and tomorrow," he told Gloria. "Grace, it's up to you to keep law and order. I will be home Monday afternoon. My cell phone is always on. I'll call you later tonight."

After the girls left for school, Rollie took Buddy for a walk around the block, stopped by Mrs. Kravitz to let her know he would be away until Monday, and then got ready to go to the airport.

•   •   •

Rollie spotted Joanna waiting at gate 23. She greeted him with a kiss and a warm hug.

"I can't believe I'm doing this," she said.

"We can't be grownups all the time," Rollie said.

"What am I supposed to do while you're working?" Joanna said.

"Be my assistant," Rollie said. "Take notes."

"I can do that," Joanna said.

"They're calling our flight," Rollie said.

•　　•　　•

After picking up their luggage, Rollie rented a car and took the highway south to Key Largo.

"You didn't tell me where we're going?" Joanna said.

"I know," Rollie said. "It's a surprise."

Thirty minutes later, Rollie pulled into the parking of Gilbert's Resort on the ocean.

"Here? We're staying here?" Joanna said.

"I know it's not much, but it's home," Rollie said.

After checking in, Rollie and Joanna went to their private cabin.

"Not too shabby," Rollie said.

"Rollie?" Joanna said.

"Yes?"

"Let's get naked."

•　　•　　•

Since the resort had twenty-four-hour services, an hour later Rollie and Joanna were having dinner poolside, as were other couples.

"I'm afraid my behavior is terrible for a forty-nine-year-old schoolteacher," Joanna said.

"But perfect for a real woman, which is what you are," Rollie said.

A waiter carried a tray with dinner to the table. He served, smiled, and went away.

"Can we try the pool after we eat?" Joanna said.

"Isn't that why we're wearing bathing suits?" Rollie said.

"What do we do tomorrow?" Joanna said.

"Go to the nursing home and talk to people about George Wendt and then the police," Rollie said.

"And I do what exactly?"

"Look professional, take notes, like that."

"You make it sound so easy," Joanna said. "So, what about this George Wendt?"

"In all likelihood he was murdered," Rollie said.

Joanna stared at Rollie for a moment. "Why?" she finally said.

"For $12,000,000," Rollie said. "It's all part of... I'll explain when we hit the pool."

A bit later, as Joanna floated on her back on top of a rubber raft, Rollie stood beside her in waist-deep water.

"So, this tontine goes back sixty years," Joanna said. "And the last one alive collects the $12,000,000."

"Correct," Rollie said.

"And your job is to prove these missing six are really missing so the last one still alive collects the money?" Joanna said.

"Also correct."

"I'm no detective, but doesn't that make the last one alive a suspect?" Joanna said.

"Ordinarily yes, but the last man standing is eighty-six years old, and the missing six are scattered all over the place," Rollie said.

"I see," Joanna said.

"I don't," Rollie said.

"I don't follow you."

"If the eighty-six-year-old man didn't murder the remaining six, then that means there is a remaining seventh that was overlooked," Rollie said.

"I get it now," Joanna said.

"Thing is, finding a murderer is not what I was hired to do," Rollie said.

"So, what are you going to do?" Joanna said.

"That depends on if you're in the mood or not," Rollie said.

Joanna hopped off the raft. "That is a definite yes," she said.

CHAPTER NINETEEN

The retirement community was like several others Rollie had recently visited in that it was structured in a large horseshoe shape all on one floor. Where it differed was in pink, stucco roofs and palm trees set in lush gardens.

As you drove south on US Route 1, if you didn't know the facility was a retirement nursing home, it would appear to be just another resort for tourists.

Key Largo is the largest of the Florida Keys at thirty-three miles long and the facility was located at the fifteen-mile marker.

Rollie turned off the highway and onto a long ramp that led to a guest parking lot.

"You didn't call ahead?" Joanna said.

"No, I never do," Rollie said. "It works best to catch them off guard."

Rollie and Joanna walked past lush grass and tall palm trees to the lobby. They entered and paused for a moment to absorb the tropical atmosphere.

They walked to the reception counter where a pleasant looking woman greeted them.

"My name is Rollie Finch and I'm a licensed private investigator from New York," Rollie said as he showed the woman his identification.

The woman read Rollie's identification and said, "A for real private investigator?"

"For real," Rollie said. "And this is my associate Joanna Kearns."

"Well, how can I help you?" the woman said.

"I've been retained by a New York law firm to investigate the disappearance of George Wendt," Rollie said.

"Oh, I see," the receptionist said. "Is there someone specific you would like to see?"

"Whoever is in charge," Rollie said.

•   •   •

Ross Neil, complex manager, looked at Rollie and Joanna from across his desk. "I'm not sure I understand why you're investigating Mr. Wendt now when he disappeared over a year ago," he said.

"Some new details have recently developed," Rollie said.

"I see," Neil said.

"What can you tell me about Mr. Wendt?" Rollie said.

Next to Rollie, Joanna had pen and notepad at the ready.

"Well, Mr. Wendt was here for a very long time," Neil said. "Years before I came along. He was at least ninety, but a healthy ninety. He participated in many activates in the complex and was well-liked by staff and other residents."

Rollie glanced at Joanna, who was jotting on her pad.

"What were his habits? What did he like to do?" Rollie said.

"I'm afraid I'll have to ask you to speak with some of our staff members on that," Neil said.

•   •   •

Hector Cruz came to Florida from Cuba forty years ago as a child.

His parents sent him to school to learn English and he spoke it with barely an accent. In his fifties now, Hector has spent the last twenty years of his life working at the retirement community.

Neil escorted Rollie and Joanna to the lunchroom where they met Cruz. After buying three cups of coffee, Neil said, "I need to get back to work."

"So, what do you want to know about Mr. Wendt?" Cruz said.

"Anything you can tell us," Rollie said.

Cruz sipped coffee and looked at Rollie. "Mr. Wendt was a fine man. The best. He was ninety, but strong as a bull. He spent his life as a lobster fisherman you know. He had arms like thick ropes. Sometimes, on movie nights, he would wheel those in wheelchairs to the theater. A ninety-year-old man doing that."

"Did he have any habits he did on a regular basis?" Rollie said.

Cruz nodded. "I'll show you," he said.

Rollie and Joanna followed Cruz to the courtyard gardens, one square acre of floral plants and palm trees. Centered in the garden was a large, round fountain. Rows of flowers grew around the perimeter.

"See those flowers there around the fountain?" Cruz said. "He planted them in his wife's memory. He would tend to them every day. Water them, prune them, feed them. One day last October, he came out to see to his flowers and that was the last anyone here ever saw of him."

Rollie looked at the blue fence that surrounded the garden.

"Is there a door in the fence?" he said.

"Two," Cruz said. "One on the east side, another on the west."

"Can I see them?" Rollie said.

Both doors were as tall as the six-foot-high fence. Each door had a new deadbolt lock. Cruz opened one door that lead directly to the guest parking lot, then the other which led to the front lawn.

"The locks were changed recently," Rollie said.

"Right after Mr. Wendt disappeared," Cruz said. "Before that you could open the locks with a paper clip."

"How often did Mr. Wendt come to the garden?" Rollie said.

"Every day except during hurricane season when a storm blew in," Cruz said. "Otherwise right after breakfast and lunch, you'd know where he'd be."

"And that day in October, he disappeared from the garden?" Rollie said.

"I assume so," Cruz said.

"Can you take us back to see Mr. Neil, please?" Rollie said.

• • •

"I'm very busy, Mr. Finch," Neil said.

"This won't take a moment," Rollie said. "I'd like to speak to the officer that investigated Mr. Wendt's disappearance. Do you have a copy of the police report?"

• • •

"We can grab some lunch before we see the police, or skip lunch and go for an early dinner," Rollie said.

"How about an early lunch and a late dinner?" Joanna said.

"Lead the way," Rollie said.

"You're the one with the car," Joanna said.

Rollie found a diner not far from the police station. Rollie and Joanna ordered the burger special and ginger ale.

"How did you do with the notes?" Rollie said.

Joanna removed her pad from her bag and handed it to Rollie.

"I didn't know people still spoke hieroglyphics," Rollie said.

"It's shorthand, silly," Joanna said. "Something they still taught in school thirty-five years ago. Greg Shorthand, to be exact."

"But I don't speak squiggle and house," Rollie said.

"Relax. I will translate word-for-word in English," Joanna said.

"Are you paid by the word?" Rollie said.

Joanna smiled. "In trade," she said.

·   ·   ·

Detective Ralph Munson was a plump man in his fifties. He sat behind his desk and looked at Rollie and Joanna. He held a file in his hand.

"After you called me, I pulled the file to refresh my memory," Munson said. "We looked for weeks for Mr. Wendt without results. It was officially listed as a missing person, but widely suspected a suicide."

"Why suicide?" Rollie said.

"A man ninety years old, living in an assisted living facility, missing his wife and son, it was a logical profile according to statistics," Munson said.

"What about his finances?" Rollie said.

"Mr. Wendt was worth north of a half million dollars," Munson said. "He was also collecting two thousand a month from social security. There was no family to leave it to, so it went to the court to decide."

"What about the facility?" Rollie said.

"It was searched thoroughly by their staff and our officers," Munson said.

"What do you think happened?" Rollie said.

"I think he waited for the right time, opened one of the doors in the garden and walked out and walked one block to the ocean and simply said good night," Munson said. "Now let me ask you why a New York City detective is so interested in a ninety-year-old missing person."

"Mr. Wendt was on a very short list to inherit $12,000,000," Rollie said.

"Well, I wish I would have known that at the time," Munson said.

"Maybe you should…" Rollie said.

"Take another look, yeah," Munson said.

CHAPTER TWENTY

As she floated on her stomach on a rubber raft in the pool, Joanna said, "So what do you do now?"

"Make my report to the attorney and turn it over to him," Rollie said. "I haven't asked, but there must be some clause in the tontine covering murder."

"And you're done?"

"Unless he wants me to continue on after I meet with the sole survivor," Rollie said.

"And will you?" Joanna said.

"I would, but I must be given a free rein to investigate as I see fit," Rollie said.

"You do have an interesting job, Rollie, I'll admit," Joanna said.

"There is another case pending, so I don't know how much time I can devote to this, but I'd like to see it through," Rollie said.

"Do you really think those six people were murdered?" Joanna said.

"No doubt in my mind," Rollie said.

"Any idea who?" Joanna said. "Besides the eighty-six-year-old man?"

"No clue at this point," Rollie said.

"Let's go to our room," Joanna said. "I feel like a warm shower and making love."

•   •   •

They opted for dinner poolside around nine o'clock.

"Dare I say I'd like to talk to you about something," Joanna said.

Rollie sipped some ginger ale and looked at Joanna over the glass.

"It's about us," Joanna said. "Our relationship."

"Before we..." Rollie said.

"Let me finish and then you can respond," Joanna said. "I like where things are going between us and I'm too old to play games, so I'll just come right out and say it. Do we have a future together?"

"Yes," Rollie said.

"That's it? Yes. That's all you got?" Joanna said.

"I'm a simple man at heart, Jo," Rollie said. "I don't believe in maybe, possibly or could be. A yes or no question gets a yes or no answer."

"So how do we proceed?" Joanna said. "I'd like to think it's as simple as you make it sound, but you live in New York and I live in South Carolina and you have three daughters and I have a mother in Florida. How does this work?"

"I'm not sure," Rollie said. "But if you want to make it work, I think we can."

"We can discuss it more over Thanksgiving," Joanna said.

"I can tell you one thing, the girls love having you around," Rollie said.

"I feel the same," Joanna said.

"So, let's just let things happen as they happen," Rollie said.

"Let's go back to our room and see if we can make something else happen," Joanna said.

"Ah, dessert," Rollie said.

•　　•　　•

Rollie had a ninety-minute layover at Charlestown before his flight to New York.

"Let's get coffee and I'll show you my notes again," Joanna said.

They entered an airport café and Joanna opened her notebook. "I'm giving you the notes in shorthand and in English," she said.

"You've been a big help," Rollie said.

"Oh posh," Joanna said.

"No, seriously," Rollie said. "It's not so easy to ask questions, make notes and remember the next question."

"Maybe we can do it again sometime?" Joanna said.

"I'd like that," Rollie said.

"Come on, I'll walk with you to your gate," Joanna said.

At Rollie's gate, they parted with a kiss. "Call me later when you get home," Joanna said.

"I will," Rollie said.

•   •   •

When Rollie entered the house the smell of freshly baked bread was in the air. He found the girls and Mrs. Kravitz in the kitchen.

"Dad's home," Gloria said and greeted Rollie with a hug.

"We're making baguettes," Grace said. "Mrs. Kravitz showed us how."

"How many?" Rollie said.

"Twelve," Giselle said.

"That is a lot of bread," Rollie said. "How are mama cat and her babies doing?"

"Come look," Gloria said.

Rollie, the girls and Mrs. Kravitz followed Rollie to his office where mama cat, her kittens and Buddy somehow managed to all fit in the bed.

"Mrs. Kravitz said she would take two," Grace said. "The other four will go to the store."

"We have to finish dinner," Gloria said. "It should be ready by seven."

"Okay," Rollie said.

After the girls and Mrs. Kravitz returned to the kitchen, Rollie called Joanna.

"Dare I say I miss you already," Joanna said.

"I was just thinking the same thing," Rollie said.

"How are the girls?"

"Fine and we have a house full of kittens," Rollie said.

"Kittens?"

Rollie told her the story and Joanna said, "What happens to mom when the kittens are gone?"

Rollie looked at Buddy and mama cat snuggling.

"Something will work out," he said.

•   •   •

Rollie ate an entire baguette with dinner. Mrs. Kravitz's recipe for beef stew was delicious, and afterward, she and the girls took Buddy for a walk around the block.

Rollie took half a baguette and a cup of coffee to his desk. Mama cat was giving her kittens a bath as he took a bite of the bread and started typing Joanna's notes into his computer.

When he was done, he read them back and decided that he would see Rose and Teal tomorrow.

Gloria came in with Buddy. As soon as he was off the leash, Buddy went to the cat bed and snuggled with the cat and kittens.

"What are we going to do when the kittens are gone, Dad?" Gloria said.

Rollie sighed. "Ask Buddy," he said.

CHAPTER TWENTY-ONE

Rose scanned the latest reports from Rollie, lowered them to his desk and looked at Rollie.

"There is no doubt in my mind that these men were murdered," Rollie said.

"I tend to agree with you, but I'm a civil attorney and have no experience in these matters," Rose said.

"Would you be open to a meeting with Gitter and Schram tomorrow?" Rollie said.

"What is it exactly you hope to accomplish?" Rose said.

"Find a murderer," Rollie said. "Save Enache from the same fate. I'm not sure at this point, but I know we can't sit by and do nothing."

"This isn't what you were hired for," Rose said.

"I know," Rollie said. "I'll submit my bill and work off the books the rest of the way, but I can't sit on my hands while someone who killed six may make it seven."

"Keep your books open," Rose said. "I can meet Gitter and Schram at two tomorrow afternoons."

"Good," Rollie said. "Bring all paperwork pertaining to the tontine including names and clauses. We need to do our homework."

"Alright," Rose said.

"See you at two," Rollie said. "Oh, and I almost forgot. Arrange for me to meet Mr. Enache as soon as possible."

.   .   .

"This must be one hell of a favor you want for you to offer a Delmonico's steak in exchange," Teal said.

"Remember I said I would tell you what I was working on when the time was right?" Rollie said.

"And I said you would do all the work and I'd take the credit," Teal said.

"Right. Well, what could be better than to start your new job with than a multiple homicide case?" Rollie said.

Slicing into his bloody steak, Teal paused. "Maybe you better start from the beginning," he said.

"Ever heard of a tontine?" Rollie said.

"A man's religion is his own business," Teal said.

"Seriously, Bill, have you?" Rollie said.

"It's some kind of old gypsy custom of saving money as a group," Teal said.

"Close enough," Rollie said.

As they ate their steaks and into dessert and coffee, Rollie told Teal everything about the Romanian tontine, the missing six and Enache.

"Two of the murders…" Rollie said.

"Alleged murders," Teal said.

"Two of the alleged murders took place in New York City and that falls under the authority of the Chief of Ds of which you are now second in command. Help me with this and that's a nice feather in your new hat."

"Bring what you have to the office and I'll take a look at it," Teal said.

"Somebody killed those men, Bill, and that somebody is still walking around just waiting to make it seven," Rollie said.

"The seventh being this old man Enache?" Teal said.

"He's the only one left," Rollie said. "Allegedly."

Teal nodded. "When can you bring what you have to the office?"

"Late tomorrow afternoon," Rollie said.

"Make it Thursday morning," Teal said. "I have a meeting with my new boss."

.　　.　　.

Rollie greeted the girls in the kitchen where they were doing homework.

"Dad, we're kind of empty in the food department," Grace said.

"Can I trust you three to go to the grocery store and not come home with a cart full of Ho Hos?" Rollie said.

"We already made a list," Grace said. "It's on the fridge."

Rollie checked the list. "Okay, head out when you're done."

"Okay, Dad," Grace said.

Rollie grabbed a can of ginger ale from the fridge and went to the office. Buddy, the cat and kittens were snuggled in the cat bed.

"Cujo you ain't, Buddy," Rollie said and took his chair. He searched through his notes and documents for a bit and then set them aside and went to his room to change into sweats.

On the way back to the office, Grace said, "We're off to the store, Dad."

"Grab $200 from my wallet and go easy on the junk food," Rollie said.

In the office, Rollie did forty-five minutes on the step climber before switching over to the Bowflex for another forty-five.

He used the workout as think-time. Somewhere in the list of one hundred names was a murderer.

Or someone who stood to gain twelve million dollars if everyone else was eliminated.

That was curtain number one and two.

What was behind curtain number three?

The only way to know for sure was to open the curtain.

CHAPTER TWENTY-TWO

Gitter filled cups with coffee and then took a seat beside Schram at the conference table in their office.

Rollie and Rose sat opposite them.

"Mr. Finch feels it necessary to treat this matter as a criminal investigation," Rose said. "And I happen to agree with him, but my experience in criminal matters is very limited."

"We have six surviving members of the tontine that I believe have been murdered to clear the path for Mr. Enache," Rollie said. "I would like to make a concentrated effort to find whoever is responsible."

"And you wish us to help?" Schram said.

"You have the resources," Rollie said.

"So do the police," Gitter said.

"And I have spoken to them and they will assist me where possible," Rollie said. "But first I need to bring them something they can work with."

"What would you like us to do?" Gitter said.

"Read every word in the formation and rules governing the tontine for anything I may have missed," Rose said. "My understanding is that if there are no surviving members to claim the money, I am to distribute it to the listed charities with discretionary powers. I need to know what I can and cannot do so I'm not criminally liable.

After all, the tontine was written sixty years ago."

"We can do that," Schram said.

"How soon?" Rollie said.

"Early next week," Gitter said.

Rose looked at Rollie.

"Good," Rollie said.

"Anything else?" Schram said.

"Give me a few days to get back to you on that," Rollie said. "Mr. Rose and I are going to visit Mr. Enache."

"Rollie, about that other case we spoke about," Gitter said.

"Call me at home tonight," Rollie said.

•   •   •

As Rollie drove across the Brooklyn Bridge, he glanced at Rose, who appeared a bit nervous.

"Mr. Rose, are you the squirrelly type?" Rollie said.

"Squirrelly?"

"The nervous type who gets paranoid easily," Rollie said.

"I consider myself a mostly calm person," Rose said. "Why do you ask?"

"Just something I'd like to run by you," Rollie said. "If something were to happen to Enache that leaves you in charge of the funds."

"That is my understanding," Rose said.

"If someone was, and I believe it to be true, killing off the tontine members and they got to Enache, they might come after you as the man holding the prize," Rollie said.

Rose looked at Rollie. "I hadn't... but that wouldn't do them any good. I'm empowered to donate the money to only designated charities."

"Charity begins at home, councilor," Rollie said. "What would

you do with a gun to your head? Would you sign the money away
or quote the bylaws of the tontine?"

Rose, suddenly appearing green in the face, slumped against his
car door window.

"Now you understand why I want criminal lawyers and the police
involved?" Rollie said.

"Yes," Rose said.

On the Brooklyn side of the bridge, Rollie checked the GPS.
"We'll be at Enache's home in less than ten minutes."

"Pull over for a moment, I need some air," Rose said.

Rollie pulled into the parking lot of a fast-food restaurant. He
and Rose got out and Rose dashed into the restaurant to use the
bathroom.

Rollie waited beside the car. Ten minutes passed and a flushed-
looking Rose finally appeared.

"Sorry for that," Rose said.

"Are you ready?" Rollie said.

"Yes."

Rollie drove the last ten minutes in silence until he parked in
front of a beautiful Park Slope townhouse.

"Enache lives here?" Rollie said.

"Yes."

"This is a million-dollar townhouse," Rollie said.

"It wasn't seventy years ago when he bought it," Rose said. "Back
then, before the movie stars and yuppies took over Park Slope it
was a working-class neighborhood."

Rollie followed Rose to the front door where Rose rang the bell.
After thirty seconds, the door opened and a pretty woman in her
mid to late twenties opened the door.

"Mr. Rose," she said.

"Hello, Abbey," Rose said. "This is Mr. Finch, the detective I told you about."

"Come in," Abbey said. "My grandfather is in the living room."

Rollie and Rose followed Abbey to the well-furnished living room where Enache sat in a wheelchair in front of the television.

A fire crackled in the fireplace.

Enache held a small glass of brandy in his right hand. "Mr. Rose, good to see you again," he said.

"This is Rollie Finch, a private detective I hired," Rose said.

Enache gave Rollie the once over and nodded. "And you've come to tell me what?" he said.

"It's a rather long and detailed story," Rollie said.

"I hope not too long. After all, I am eighty-six years old," Enache said.

Rollie smiled. "I'll do my best to keep it short," he said.

"Abigail, could you make some coffee for our guests?" Enache said.

"Yes, grandfather," Abbey said and went to the kitchen.

"Please have a seat," Enache said.

Rollie and Rose took seats on the sofa beside the fire.

"At my age, my bones get cold," Enache said. "A good fire and a glass of brandy take the chill off."

The room was quite warm, and Rollie loosened his tie.

"Were you a cop, Mr. Finch? You have that look," Enache said.

"Twenty-three years," Rollie said.

"Mr. Finch retired as a lieutenant in Homicide," Rose said.

Enache looked at Rollie. "That makes you more than a dumb beat cop," he said.

Abbey returned with a tray loaded with a coffee pot, cups, cream and sugar.

"I would be lost without her," Enache said.

"Grandfather, I have to take a run to the market and then the pharmacy for your medicine," Abbey said. "I won't be long."

"Take your time, dear. I'm in for a long story," Enache said as Abbey left the room.

Rollie filled two cups with coffee and gave one to Rose.

"I take pills for my blood pressure, heart, gout and tremors," Enache said. "Oh, I can walk, but the doctors are fearful I'll get the shakes, fall and kill myself."

"Mr. Enache, I would…" Rollie said.

Enache tossed back his brandy and said, "Would you be so kind as to pour me another."

Rollie stood, took the glass, walked to the bar across the room, filled the glass with brandy and returned to Enache.

"Thank you," Enache said.

Rollie took his seat on the sofa.

"You're here about the tontine," Enache said.

"Yes," Rollie said.

"I was a miserable fucking human being for most of my life," Enache said.

"Mr. Enache…" Rollie said.

"Rotten to the core I was," Enache said. "I cheated on my first wife with my second and my second wife with my mistress who became my third. I cheated at business and stole from my partners and when they lost everything, I didn't give a shit."

"Mr. Enache, I…" Rollie said.

"I was in the jewelry business with two Jews who assumed I was also Jewish," Enache said. "I cheated them out of every nickel I could get and forced them to sell their interest in our store and when they lost everything, I didn't give a shit. I had one son by my second wife and treated him like crap. He died twenty years ago in a car accident along with his wife."

Enache paused to sip some brandy.

"Abigail changed me, changed my life," Enache said. "Suddenly I was charged with raising this three-year-old girl and everything changed. I retired and sold the business and dedicated my life to raising her the way I should have raised my son."

Rollie sipped coffee.

Rose sipped coffee.

"She went to Brooklyn Tech College when she could have gone anywhere she wanted, so she could stay here and take care of me," Enache said. "I made a good amount of money when I sold the business and social security chips in another $2,000 a month, so we are comfortable at the moment."

Enache sipped some brandy. Rollie waited for Enache to either get to a point or talk himself out.

"However, in my greed to live, I'm afraid I have done my granddaughter a disservice," Enache said. "You see, because taking care of me is a full-time job, Abigail has never entered the work force. Despite her college education, she's never even so much as had a part time job. I have to ask myself what will happen to her after I'm gone."

Enache's ramblings suddenly became clear to Rollie. He was concerned for his granddaughter's future after he was gone.

"So, you see, I have to live long enough to collect the tontine money so I can ensure Abigail is taken care of for the rest of her life," Enache said.

"Did you know you were in line for the tontine money prior to Mr. Rose contacting you?" Rollie said.

"To be honest I hadn't thought of it in decades," Enache said. "I never kept in touch with most of the members and honestly, who expects to live to eighty-six."

"At the moment, as far as we can determine you are the only one left," Rollie said. "However, there is a problem."

Enache looked at Rollie.

"Six surviving members appear to have been murdered," Rollie said. "That's going to require some investigation."

"Mr. Rose, does that disqualify me from inheriting the money?" Enache said.

"It does not," Rose said.

"Unless of course, you murdered them," Rollie said.

Enache looked at Rollie and laughed. "Do I look capable of murder to you?" he said.

"Anybody, under the right circumstances and at the right time is capable of just about anything," Rollie said.

"That's a cop talking," Enache said. "But if it will make you feel better, the only thing I have ever killed is my own soul."

"You're not seeing the bigger picture," Rollie said. "If someone else has murdered those six, you might be next with your granddaughter in the way."

Enache stared at Rollie and Rollie could see Enache doing the math in his head.

"Oh my God," Enache said. "No, not my Abigail. Rose, you do something about this. Nothing can happen to my granddaughter."

"We are doing something about it, Mr. Enache," Rose said. "Mr. Finch is investigating, and he has many connections with the police."

"Wait," Enache said. "If I'm killed, who gets the money?"

"That is what we are trying to find out," Rollie said.

"How… how were they killed?" Enache said.

"We don't know," Rollie said. "They disappeared from their retirement homes and condos. Police listed them as missing persons because they had no way of knowing they were related through the tontine."

"Should I hire a live-in bodyguard?" Enache said.

"At least until you collect the tontine money," Rollie said. "I can recommend someone I know from the police department."

"Yes, please call him," Enache said.

"Right now?" Rollie said.

"I won't have Abigail in danger for one single moment," Enache said.

"Give me ten minutes," Rollie said.

• • •

Rollie sat on the front steps of Enache's townhouse and called Bo Redford on his cell phone. Rollie wanted the privacy and fresh air after being in that overheated den for half an hour.

Redford answered his phone with, "Redford Security."

"Bo, Rollie Finch," Rollie said.

"Rollie, how the hell are you?" Redford said.

"Good. Got a job for you if you're available," Rollie said.

"I'm available," Redford said. "How many men?"

"I was thinking just you," Rollie said. "It's a live-in baby-sitting job for an old man."

"Where?"

"You still live in Brooklyn?" Rollie said.

"Coney Island."

"Take down this address," Rollie said.

• • •

Bo Redford stood six-foot-three and was built like a linebacker. He retired at the age of forty-five after twenty-two years on the police department, going out as a detective in Robbery and Vice.

He started the security company six years ago with several other retired police officers and they specialized in bodyguard work.

Rollie met Redford in front of Enache's brownstone where Rollie explained the situation to him and then brought Redford inside to meet Enache and Rose.

"You certainly look up to the mark, Mr. Redford," Enache said. "Any questions?"

"As I understand it, you need personal protection until such time as you inherit a large sum of money from a tontine," Redford said. "The timeline if anywhere from thirty to sixty days depending upon Rollie's investigation into possible murders of some of the tontine members."

"My granddaughter is the priority," Enache said. "I am pretty much a worthless old man, but Abigail has her entire life ahead of her. Is that understood?"

"It is," Redford said.

"When can you start?" Enache said.

"Right now," Redford said.

"Mr. Finch tells me you charge three thousand a week for live-in protection," Enache said. "When Abigail returns, I'll have her write you a check for at least one month."

．　　●　　●

"I don't understand any of this," Abbey said.

"Mr. Finch, would you do the explaining?" Enache said.

"Abigail let's go to the kitchen and talk," Rollie said. "Mr. Rose, please join us."

In the kitchen, Abbey poured coffee into three cups at the table.

"Your grandfather's life and your own may be in serious danger," Rollie said.

"From what?" Abbey said.

"Well, I'll tell you," Rollie said and explained the situation to Abigail.

"Oh my God," Abbey said. "Why didn't grandfather tell me all this?"

"He's only known he was in line for it a short period of time and he wanted to surprise you," Rollie said. "He didn't know about the danger until today."

"And this man has to stay in our house?" Abbey said.

"Bo Redford is a retired police officer who now specializes in protection," Rollie said. "He'll be here round the clock to safeguard you and your grandfather until this is resolved."

"How long is that?" Abbey said.

"Forty-five days, maybe longer," Rollie said. "It depends on how things progress."

"What if I need to go to the store or pharmacy for grandfather?" Abbey said.

"You don't go alone," Rollie said. "I'll speak to Paul about that."

"This whole thing is very scary," Abbey said.

"I know, but we will get you and your grandfather through this," Rollie said. "Alright, let's go meet your new roommate."

•　　　•　　　•

Before leaving, Rollie met privately with Redford in the hallway.

"How serious is this threat?" Redford said.

"I believe six have been killed so far, that serious," Rollie said.

"Who is doing the killing?" Redford said.

"That's the twelve-million-dollar question," Rollie said.

"If the old man is the last one in line, who gets the money if he's dead?" Redford said.

"Nobody," Rollie said. "It goes to charity."

"This doesn't make sense," Redford said.

"Not yet," Rollie said.

"By the way, great job on that Knox thing, the scumbag," Redford said.

"Thanks. Call me at least once a day," Rollie said.

"Sure. Free room and board and a fat check, I'll call you twice a day," Redford said.

"I have to drive Rose back to his office," Rollie said.

"Hey, how is old Bill these days?" Redford said.

"He's the new Assistant Chief of Ds," Rollie said.

"I knew he'd make good."

"He did."

"Talk to you later," Redford said.

CHAPTER TWENTY-THREE

"Paul was a good cop alright," Teal said. "He'll get the job done."

"If I thought otherwise, I wouldn't have called him," Rollie said.

"This whole thing is very confusing," Teal said. "If the old man didn't kill those missing six, which is highly unlikely and he is next in line to be killed, who is doing the killing and why?"

"That's a good question, Bill," Rollie said. "And that's where you come in."

"I was wondering when you'd get around to that one," Teal said.

"John Henry Rose Jr.," Rollie said. "Find out everything you can about him for me, would you."

"Isn't he the lawyer that hired you?" Teal said.

"He also stands to gain controlling interest of twelve million dollars if Enache dies before he collects," Rollie said.

"Well that's interesting," Teal said.

"Look at everything you can," Rollie said. "And also look at Victor Enache."

"The old man?"

Rollie nodded. "His finances, everything."

"Give me a day and I'll see what I can come up with," Teal said.

"I have to go home," Rollie said.

•   •   •

Gloria and Mrs. Kravitz were baking an apple pie when Rollie walked into the kitchen.

"Something smells good," he said.

"Mrs. Kravitz has a secret recipe for apple pie," Gloria said.

"And dinner?"

"She's got that covered, too," Gloria said.

"Then you'll be joining us," Rollie said.

"I wasn't…" Mrs. Kravitz said.

"She'll stay," Gloria said.

"Good. I'm going to change and then go to my office," Rollie said.

Rollie went to his bedroom and changed into slacks and a pullover shirt, returned to the kitchen for a can of ginger ale and then went to the office.

Buddy, the cat and her kittens were curled up in the cat bed. Buddy looked up at him for a moment, but the snooty cat did not so much as budge.

Rollie took his chair at the desk and called Joanna on his cell phone.

"I was hoping you would call," Joanna said.

"Been busy with this case," Rollie said. "If your flight booked?"

"Yes. I arrive at noon on Wednesday," Joanna said. "Leave Sunday night at seven."

"The girls and I have some surprises for you," Rollie said.

"I love surprises," Joanna said.

"Dress warm," Rollie said. "It's not a South Carolina winter."

After chatting for a bit, Rollie hung up and waited for the hardline phone to ring. While he waited, he made detailed notes of the day's activities.

Around 6:30, Schram called on the hard-line phone.

"What the hell was that all about in the office today?" Schram said.

"Cop paranoia," Rollie said.

"You don't trust Rose?"

"As a cop I trust nobody."

"That's a poor attitude, Rollie," Schram said.

"A good detective can't trust anybody until they prove trustworthy," Rollie said.

"And Rose hasn't?"

"Not yet."

"Us?"

"If I didn't think you trustworthy, I wouldn't work for you," Rollie said.

"That's good to know," Schram said.

"So how are you doing with the tontine bylaws?" Rollie said.

"You'll be happy to know there aren't any statutes governing the formation of a tontine," Schram said. "Mostly because ninety-five percent of the country never even heard of it."

"So, what does that mean to us?" Rollie said.

"We aren't done yet with our research, but the tontine bylaws were written and witnessed by Rose Senior and a judge and they seem to be binding," Schram said.

"So if Enache dies before he collects, Rose gains control of the money," Rollie said.

"Appears so," Schram said. "And the tontine doesn't say which charity and when he is to designate the funds."

"So he could hold onto the funds for ten years before releasing the twelve million and keep the million in interest for himself?" Rollie said.

"Nothing says he can't," Schram said. "The tontine ends when the last person collects or dies and the amount gets locked in. Interest was never taken into account past the due date."

"And you wonder why I'm skeptical," Rollie said.

"We'll finish the research tomorrow," Schram said. "Now about Marks? When can you meet with him?"

"Friday afternoon okay?" Rollie said.

"We'll set it up," Schram said. "Say two o'clock?"

"I'll be there," Rollie said.

After hanging up with Schram, Rollie called Bo Redford.

"How's it going, Bo?" Rollie said.

"Quiet," Redford said. "The old man and the girl are having dinner in the dining room. I took the bedroom on the first floor so I'd be closer to a break in if the worst happens. Rollie, do you really think the old guy is in serious danger?"

"Ask the other six in line that disappeared," Rollie said.

"I guess you never know," Redford said. "I made arrangements with one of my part time people to take the girl shopping when she needs to go out."

"Call me every day with a report unless something happens, then call immediately," Rollie said.

"Will do," Redford said.

Done with his calls, Rollie went to the kitchen to find dinner on the table, Grace and Giselle home and Mrs. Kravitz about to serve stuffed peppers.

"I was just about to come get you, Dad," grace said.

Rollie took his usual chair. "So, who had a better day than I did?" he said.

· · ·

After dinner, everybody went to the garage to check on the kittens.

Mrs. Kravitz held two of them and said, "These two are mine. Just look at these little darlings."

Buddy, upset with two kittens being away from their mother, sat beside Mrs. Kravitz and whined softly.

"I best put them back before Buddy blows a gasket," Mrs. Kravitz said.

"Get the leash, Gloria," Rollie said. "We'll take Buddy for a spin while your sisters do the dishes."

Into the third week of November, the night air was dipping below forty degrees and Gloria dressed Buddy in his sweater and wool boots.

"Dad, we've been talking about something," Gloria said.

"Who is we and what's the something?" Rollie said.

"We is your daughters and the something is the cat," Gloria said.

"And what about the cat?" Rollie said.

"Well, after the kittens are all gone it seems cruel to Buddy to get rid of the cat seeing as how attached he is to her," Gloria said.

"Like I didn't see that coming," Rollie said.

"Is that a yes or a no?" Gloria said.

"Ask Buddy," Rollie said.

CHAPTER TWENTY-FOUR

Rollie was up before the girls and prepared them a full breakfast.

"I'm home today, so I'll take Buddy for his walk," Rollie said.

"We'll be home around three thirty," Grace said.

After the girls left for school, Rollie did the breakfast dishes and then took a mug of coffee to his office. Ever diligent, Buddy watched over mama cat and her kittens as she gave them a bath.

Rollie read the notes he wrote yesterday and then typed them into a case document in his computer.

Just before noon, Gitter called.

"We finished researching the tontine bylaws," Gitter said. "Adam was correct in what he told you yesterday. Rose gains control of the funds if there are no survivors and although it states the money goes to charity, there is no time frame for the donation."

"So there is nothing to stop him from holding the funds for ten years and keeping a million in interest for himself?" Rollie said.

"Not a thing," Schram said. "It never occurred to anybody sixty years ago that this situation might happen."

"I doubt it will again," Rollie said.

"Two o'clock tomorrow for Marks," Gitter said.

"I'll be there," Rollie said.

After hanging up with Gitter, Rollie went for Buddy's leash and his jacket. Just as he was tossing on the jacket, Mrs. Kravitz rang the doorbell.

"I wasn't sure if you were home," she said. "Buddy needs his walk."

"We can go together," Rollie said.

The temperature was in the mid fifties and Buddy didn't need his sweater. Rollie and Mrs. Kravitz took Buddy for a long walk around the block.

"What happens to the cat after the kittens are gone?" Mrs. Kravitz said.

"Buddy has decided to keep her," Rollie said.

"Buddy has?"

"Try and separate them," Rollie said.

"I made some dark chocolate brownies for the girls for after school," Mrs. Kravitz said.

When they reached home, Rollie said, "Would you like to come in and see your kittens?"

"I would actually," Mrs. Kravitz said.

While Mrs. Kravitz sat in Rollie's chair with her two kittens on her lap, Rollie brought in two cups of coffee.

"Since my daughter and son moved to Florida and California, I don't see my grandkids much anymore," Mrs. Kravitz said. "These two little beauties will help with the loneliness I feel sometimes."

"That reminds me," Rollie said. "The girls asked me to invite you to Thanksgiving dinner, if you have no other plans."

"You're a terrible liar and I accept," Mrs. Kravitz said. "Provided you let me help with the dinner."

"When you bring the girls your brownies, you can plan the menu with them," Rollie said.

After Mrs. Kravitz went home, Rollie changed into sweats and did thirty minutes on the step climber and another thirty on the Bowflex machine.

He let his thoughts wander.

If Enache was behind the murders, and the chances were slim to none, how would he prove it?

If Rose was behind it, why bother to bring in a private detective to prolong Enache's life?

If not Enache, if not Rose, then who?

A seventh man?

Operating behind the scenes, waiting for all others to be eliminated before he steps into the light to claim the prize.

After his last set on the Bowflex, before he went for a shower, Rollie called Teal on his cell phone.

"If you're calling about Rose, I'm still checking," Teal said.

"Come to dinner tomorrow and bring the results," Rollie said.

"I smell a rat," Teal said.

"What you'd smell is home cooking lovingly prepared by my three beautiful daughters," Rollie said.

"You're an evil man, Rollie," Teal said. "You know the diet my wife has me on."

"Carrot sticks and lettuce leaves, or real food and dessert," Rollie said. "Your choice."

"What time?"

"Seven thirty."

"I'll be there."

"And bring the results."

"I'm walking into a trap, aren't I?" Teal said.

"Think warm apple pie with ice cream," Rollie said.

"You're a rat bastard, Rollie."

"Seven thirty," Rollie said and hung up.

Rollie went for a shower and changed into a clean warm-up suit and met the girls and Mrs. Kravitz in the kitchen.

"Dad, brownies," Gloria said.

"Brownies, then homework, then we'll take Buddy for a spin around the block," Rollie said. "Oh, and your Uncle Bill is coming for dinner tomorrow. Oh, and Mrs. Kravitz is coming for Thanksgiving, so start preparing now."

Rollie grabbed a brownie. "I'll be in the office," he said.

CHAPTER TWENTY-FIVE

Rollie spent the day brushing up on Robert Marks. The fifty-three-year-old self-made billionaire looked guilty as hell at first glance.

Fingerprints on the hunting knife that killed his wife, his much younger wife that was soon to be ex number four.

Blood on his right hand and fingerprints on the knife and blood on his right knee didn't look promising.

The divorce was going to get ugly and messy in the media.

Marks could well afford the one hundred million he'd have to pay his wife for the divorce. What he couldn't afford was a scandal when he had a new hotel and golf course opening and a new building in Manhattan and another in Miami about to open.

The publicity of another messy divorce was bad for business.

So, to avoid the bad publicity, what does Marks do but come home and stab his wife to death in the living room of his twenty-five-million-dollar penthouse apartment on Fifth Avenue.

On any level that didn't make sense.

A man like Marks could pay to have any publicity squelched.

Murdering your wife to avoid bad publicity did not make a whole lot of sense.

At 11:30, Rollie stopped by Mrs. Kravitz's house to tell her Gloria would be over after school, and then he drove into Manhattan.

•   •   •

Rollie met Gitter and Schram and Robert Marks in the conference room at two o'clock. Gitter and Schram wore their usual impeccable suits, but Marks was dressed for a construction site.

When Marks stood up, he was about six-foot five-inches tall, made two inches taller by his work boots.

"I didn't kill my wife," Marks said.

"I didn't say you did," Rollie said.

"I just want it on record with you," Marks said. "They told me about you, what you did with that scumbag Knox. I don't want you to think I'm like him. I'm not."

Rollie took a chair opposite Marks at the desk.

"So, tell me what happened," Rollie said.

"I spent the day at a construction site on 43rd and Third Avenue," Marks said. "I came home and she was dead. I called 911 and was arrested. That's all I know."

"That kind of explanation will get you twenty-five to life," Rollie said. "I need more if I'm to investigate this."

"That's all there is," Marks said. "When I saw her there on the floor, I called 911. I don't remember much else. That's the truth."

Rollie opened the file that Gitter and Schram had set on the table and searched through the crime scene photographs. Then he scanned the crime scene and forensic reports.

"It says that your wife was five-feet eight-inches tall," Rollie said.

"That's right," Marks said.

"How tall are you?" Rollie said.

"Six-five."

"And with those boots, about six-seven," Rollie said. "Were you wearing construction boots that day?"

"I told you I was on a construction site that day," Marks said.

"The forensic report says that she was stabbed at a downward angle of forty-five degrees," Rollie said.

"So?" Marks said.

"Stand up," Rollie said as he picked up a pencil from the table and stood.

Marks stood.

"The forensics report says she was stabbed through the heart at a downward angle of forty-five degrees," Rollie said. "That means the killer held the knife above his head and stabbed downward."

"What are you getting at?" Marks said.

"Take this pencil and stab downward at me," Rollie said.

Marks took the pencil. He held it above his head and stabbed downward at Rollie and stopped just short of hitting Rollie on the top of the head.

"Now bend at the knees about a foot or so and do it again," Rollie said.

Marks bent his knees and stabbed at Rollie again and the pencil lined up with the center of his chest.

"I would say the killer was much shorter than you, Mr. Marks," Rollie said. "Around my height. Wouldn't you agree?"

Gitter and Schram looked at Rollie.

"The forensics says the knife was a hunting knife," Rollie said. "Ever own one, Mr. Marks?"

"No."

"Where was the knife when you found your wife's body?" Rollie said.

"Right next to her," Marks said.

"Right side, left side, where?" Rollie said.

"Right side next to her head," Marks said.

"How did you get blood on your right knee and right hand?" Rollie said.

"I don't remember," Marks said.

"Drop the pencil," Rollie said.

Marks dropped the pencil.

"Now kneel down and pick it up," Rollie said.

Marks got down on his right knee and picked up the pencil with his right hand.

"That's how you got blood on your right knee and right hand," Rollie said.

Marks looked up at Rollie.

"They said you were good," Marks said as he stood. "But how do you prove this?"

"We don't need to prove it," Gitter said. "We just need to put doubt in the minds of the jury."

Marks nodded. "I have to get back to work now," he said.

After Marks left, Schram said, "Thank you, Rollie. Excellent as always."

"Let me get that report on the tontine," Rollie said.

"Sure," Schram said.

They went to Gitter's office where he gave Rollie a folder.

"Once Rose gains control of the funds there is nothing to stop him from releasing them or holding onto them for as long as he wishes," Schram said.

"Thanks," Rollie said.

"No, thank you, Rollie," Gitter said. "Drop by next week for the witness list."

CHAPTER TWENTY-SIX

Rollie and Gloria set the filet mignon steaks to marinate in the refrigerator and then got started making an apple pie from scratch.

They used the recipe from the book Gloria's mother wrote in pen. She would put stars next to a recipe to indicate her satisfaction with it. The apple pie recipe had four stars.

After the pie was done, they set it on the counter to cool and then took Buddy for a walk around the block.

Later, Rollie was heating the backyard grill when Grace and Giselle came home from their job at the pet store.

"We got our first paycheck today," Grace said. "Dad, look at the taxes they took."

"Get used to it, honey," Rollie said. "It only gets worse."

"Can we help with anything?" Giselle said. "We can do our homework Saturday night."

"Help Gloria set the table is about all," Rollie said.

By the time Teal arrived at 7:30, Rollie had the steaks sizzling nicely on the grill.

"Mashed potatoes, carrots, sweet potatoes, biscuits and steak… you must want something pretty big," Teal said as he watched Rollie flip the steaks.

"Remember our deal?" Rollie said. "I do the work; you get the glory."

"I remember," Teal said.

"Steaks are done, let's eat," Rollie said.

Over dinner, Grace and Giselle told Teal about their jobs and complained about the taxes taken from their paychecks.

"Get used to paying taxes, girls," Teal said. "They'll be with you the rest of your life."

"That's what Dad said," Grace said.

"Dad is wise," Teal said.

After dinner, Rollie and Teal went to his office.

Teal looked at the cat bed. "That is not normal cat and dog behavior," he said.

"I'm afraid I'm stuck with the cat," Rollie said.

"What about the kittens?" Teal said.

"Two are going to a neighbor, four to the pet store for adoption," Rollie said. "Now about the…"

"Let me see," Teal said.

He walked to the cat bed and squatted down. Buddy looked at him as if to say hands off.

"It's alright, boy. I won't hurt them," Teal said and picked up a kitten.

Carrying the kitten to Rollie's desk, Teal took the chair. "That's a good kitty," he said as he gently petted it.

"About the report…" Rollie said.

Grace entered the office. "Apple pie is all warmed up. I didn't know you liked cats, Uncle Bill."

"My wife loves them," Teal said. "In fact, I think I'll take two for her birthday which is in early January."

"Really?" Grace said.

"This one and one other," Teal said.

"Come on, pie is ready," Grace said.

Teal put the kitten back in the bed, and Grace took Teal's hand and led him to the kitchen.

Rollie sighed and followed.

Teal's slice of pies was about a quarter of the entire pie and he ate it with a large scoop of vanilla ice cream on top.

"Girls, I'm stuffed," Teal said.

"We made coffee for you," Grace said.

Rollie and Teal took mugs of coffee back to the office.

"The report?" Rollie said.

Teal removed a thick envelope from his suit jacket pocket and handed it to Rollie. "Now that you bribed me with dinner and pie, maybe you'll tell me why I'm here."

"I've been trying to for the past hour," Rollie said.

Teal picked up his kitten and sat in Rollie's chair. "I'm listening," he said.

"If Enache didn't get rid of the missing six and Rose isn't behind it, then one of the tontine members could still be alive and a serial murderer," Rollie said. "A serial killer is a nice feather in your new cap."

"And how do you propose to find him?" Teal said.

"Social security," Rollie said.

"What?"

"If someone is drawing a check every month it means they are still alive," Rollie said. "You're the Assistant Chief of Detectives. Get a judge to issue a warrant and check the one hundred names except for Enache."

Teal sighed. "Damn that detective brain of yours always making work for me," he said. "You have the list?"

Rollie picked up an envelope from his desk and handed it to Teal. "This will have to wait until Monday," he said.

"I know," Rollie said. "Try to have it ready by Tuesday."

"Tuesday of next year," Teal said.

"Buddy wants his kitten back," Rollie said.

Teal returned the kitten to the cat bed. "My wife will love two kittens for her birthday," he said.

"I'll walk you out," Rollie said.

At Teal's car, Rollie said, "Thanks for the report on Rose."

"Don't thank me until you read it," Teal said.

"Can I thank you in advance for the Tontine list of names?" Rollie said.

"Dinner covered that," Teal said.

"I'll call you after I read the report," Rollie said.

After Teal left, Rollie went to the kitchen where the girls were tidying up.

"Dad, we can sleep late tomorrow," Grace asked. "We don't have to be at work until noon."

"Feel up to a video game?" Giselle said.

"You and Giselle against me and the squirt," Grace said.

"Loser makes breakfast," Giselle said.

Rollie looked at Grace. "I guess you and the squirt are making breakfast," he said.

CHAPTER TWENTY-SEVEN

After Rollie and Giselle made breakfast, Giselle got Grace and Gloria out of bed.

"What did you losers make?" Grace said.

"Belgium waffles with bacon and you only won because dad never played that game before," Giselle said.

At the breakfast table, Grace said, "Dad, can Giselle and I go to the movies tomorrow with James and Alex? We can pay our own way now."

"The boys pick you up here and have you home by eleven. Agreed?" Rollie said.

"Agreed," Grace said.

"And now for the other thing," Rollie said.

"What other thing?" Grace said.

"You both have savings accounts, which up until now have been supported by your allowance," Rollie said. "I'm going to suggest that you each deposit one hundred dollars each payday. Agreed?"

"Agreed," Giselle said.

After breakfast, Grace and Giselle dressed for work and left early so they could go to the bank.

Rollie and Gloria took Buddy for a walk around the block.

"I have some work to do, but if you want, we can take Buddy to the dog park around three," Rollie said.

"Sure," Gloria said.

"Don't look so glum, I didn't forget your allowance," Rollie said.

"Do I have to put mine in the bank?" Gloria said.

"Ten percent," Rollie said.

"Deal."

.   .   .

While Buddy snuggled in with the cat and kittens, Rollie sat at his desk with a mug of coffee and opened the folder Teal left on Rose.

Rose had just turned sixty-one.

"Happy birthday," Rollie said aloud.

Rose grew up in the townhouse he still occupied. His residence was on the second and third floors, while the office occupied the first. He lived on the third floor while his parents lived on the second.

He went to NYU Law School, so had no reason to move out as it was a short walk to class every day.

After graduating law school, Rose went to work for his father. After his parents died, Rose took over the firm.

His average income was $200,000 a year, give or take. He has a nest egg savings account worth $1,000,000. His father purchased a summer cottage in New Hampshire that Rose still owned.

Twenty thousand in a checking account. No outstanding credit cards. No life insurance as he had no one to leave it to.

The townhouse was worth around $3,000,000 and was paid off decades ago by his father.

Rose could retire comfortably if he wanted.

But with an extra million come due in ten years that retirement would be that much better.

However, there was nothing in Rose's history that said he was dishonest in any way. In fact, he still charged client fees the same amount for the past ten years.

Rose did own a gun, a .38 revolver, which he purchased legally twenty years ago. The report didn't say if he still owned it.

He never married, but there was nothing to indicate he was homosexual.

If you judged Rose by his life, there was no reason to suspect him of murder and extortion.

But a million dollars changes things.

Rollie knew many a criminal who did the worst for far less.

•   •   •

Rollie found Gloria in the kitchen where she was getting ready to cook dinner for tonight.

"Dog park?" Rollie said.

"Dog park," Gloria said.

The afternoon was warm—around fifty-five degrees—and they played Frisbee with Buddy for about an hour.

When Buddy had enough, Gloria said, "Can we stop by the market for a few things I'll need for dinner."

"What's on the menu?" Rollie said.

"Something I found in Mom's recipe book," Gloria said.

Rollie drove to the grocery store a few blocks from the dog park.

"I need forty dollars," Gloria said. "You can wait here with Buddy."

"Yes, ma'am," Rollie said.

While Gloria was in the market, Rollie called Redford on his cell phone.

Hi, Rollie," Redford said.

"How's it going?" Rollie said.

"One of my men took the girl to the grocery store and pharmacy," Redford said. "The old man is taking a nap before dinner."

"Sounds uneventful," Rollie said.

"Rollie, the old man, he's a talker," Redford said. "He's got a million stories about how he screwed so many people in business. He says he wants to make things right with the tontine money."

"How?"

"He says he wants to give his granddaughter half," Redford said. "And a million each to the families of his ex business partners and the rest to charity."

"It sounds like redemption is what he's looking for," Rollie said.

"Yeah, a seat at the table in the great by and by," Redford said.

"Call if…" Rollie said.

Will do," Redford said.

Gloria returned with two bags of groceries and a dollar seventy-five in change.

"So, what's on the menu?" Rollie said.

"It's a surprise," Gloria said.

"That could go either way," Rollie said.

"If it turns out bad, blame it on mom," Gloria said.

•   •   •

Rollie read the report on Rose again as he sipped ginger ale from the can.

Rose was not physically capable of killing anybody, much less six. He would have to hire out to get it done.

Rollie checked Rose's finances again. There were no withdrawals from his savings account and no large amounts checks written. If he paid a professional to kill six people it would cost at least a hundred thousand.

It was possible he kept a stash that large in his house in undeclared income, but highly unlikely.

That opened up the idea of a partner.

Someone willing to murder six and possibly seven for the prize.

The question was who?

Rollie let his thoughts run wild for a moment. Say Rose contacted a living member of the tontine, a man still young enough to enjoy the money. Rose contacts the man and they arrange for a split of the money, say ten million for the man and two for Rose.

Given the fact that it was Rose who hired Rollie and agreed to protect Enache, that scenario was highly unlikely.

Rollie quit thinking when Joanna called on the hard-line phone.

"I'll be there in nine days," Joanna said.

"We're on pins and needles," Rollie said. "The girls are planning all kinds of things."

"I planned a few things of my own," Joanna said.

"Oh. Like?"

"Like a surprise isn't one if you know in advance," Joanna said.

"Can I get a hint?"

"It's small enough to bring on the plane," Joanna said.

"That could be anything."

"It could."

They chatted for a bit and then Rollie went to the kitchen.

"Something smells pretty good," Rollie said.

"That's the garlic rolls," Gloria said. "I hope I timed this right. They should be home in a few minutes."

Shortly before six pm, Grace and Giselle came home from the pet store.

"Something smells good," Grace said.

"Garlic rolls," Rollie said.

"Dinner in fifteen minutes," Gloria said.

134

After Grace and Giselle changed, Gloria took two large pizzas from the oven and set them on the countertop to cool.

"Mom's recipe," Gloria said. "Bacon, burger and broccoli and garlic rolls made from scratch."

"Can we help with anything?" Grace said.

"No, but you can eat," Gloria said.

CHAPTER TWENTY-EIGHT

As Rose wasn't a criminal lawyer, the odds on him encountering a professional hit man were slim to none.

On the other hand, he was a lawyer and lawyers knew people. It was possible Rose was able to find a hit man for hire through his legal connections.

It was also possible, though highly unlikely that he kept a large amount of undeclared money in his townhouse.

The more he thought about it the less likely a suspect Rose became. If he intended to kill Enache for the money, why bother to hire Rollie and then agree to protection?

The idea of a seventh man was looking more and more plausible. Except that how would the seventh man know who died and where the survivors lived?

Rollie opened the file on the tontine by laws.

According to the agreement, every time a member dies, written notification must be sent to Rose and recorded.

Rose knew the location of every member dead or alive.

Except, on the surface he wanted Enache alive, so how does Rose benefit?

Motive.

It always came down to motive.

Reasons for murder include lust, love, revenge, hatred, power and money. Lust, love, revenge, hatred and power were out, so that left just money.

Rollie left the office to change into sweats. Gloria, Grace and Giselle were doing homework at the kitchen table.

"What time is the movie?" Rollie said.

"Seven fifteen," Grace said. "James and Alex will be here at six. We're taking my car."

"What about dinner?" Rollie said.

"Burgers at the diner," Grace said. "Girls pay for the movie; boys pay for burgers."

"Home by eleven," Rollie said. "Tomorrow is school."

Rollie returned to the office, checked on Buddy, the cat and kittens, and then did thirty minutes on the step climber.

Motive?

Money.

If Enache died before collecting the twelve million, Rose gets control of the tontine and can sit on the funds for as long as he liked and collected a fortune in interest.

If Enache lived and collected the twelve million, Rose got nothing except his feel for handling the tontine.

Yet Rose took every precaution to ensure Enache stayed alive to collect the money.

Why?

After thirty minutes on the step climber, Rollie switched out to the Bowflex machine.

Why?

What if... Rose and Enache entered into an agreement that if Enache won the tontine... Enache would split the prize with Rose?

Rollie paused and sat up on the bench.

So... Rose devised an elaborate plan to eliminate Enache's competition ensuring Enache the winner.

Except how did Rose eliminate the missing six?

Rollie continued his workout on the Bowflex.

Money wasn't the root of all evil, but the greed for it was.

Workout finished, Rollie went to his bedroom to take a shower.

Somehow Rose managed to pull it off and eliminate six people. The question was how?

Rollie changed into slacks and a long sleeve sweatshirt and went to the kitchen. Gloria was alone at the table.

"They're getting ready for their date," Gloria said.

"Are you done with your homework?" Rollie said.

"Yes, just double checking it," Gloria said.

"Check it later, Buddy needs his walk," Rollie said.

Rollie and Gloria took Buddy for a stroll around the block. Gloria held the leash while Buddy did his sniffing, tugging, and peeing.

As they passed Mrs. Kravitz's house, Gloria said, "You know something, Dad. I've always thought of old people as slow and tired all the time, but I can hardly keep up with Mrs. Kravitz. She has so much energy and she's seventy-nine."

"Some older people will surprise you, honey," Rollie said. "What do you say you and I eat out tonight while your sisters are out with their knot heads?"

"Only if you twist my arm," Gloria said.

Back in his office, Rollie took a mug of coffee to his desk and thought for a while.

"…but I can hardly keep up with Mrs. Kravitz. She has so much energy and she's seventy-nine," Gloria had said.

Suppose Enache had the same energy and drive and decided to take matters into his own hands, possibly even teaming up with Rose to split the prize money?

By his own accounts, Enache lived his life as a liar and a cheat and as the old cliché says, leopards don't change their spots.

Supposing Enache approached Rose with the idea of eliminating all others and splitting the prize between them?

It fit.

It fit like an old glove.

But a plausible theory was a far cry from evidence and proof.

"Hey, Dad," Gloria said as she poked her head into the office. "The nincompoops are here."

Rollie and Gloria went to the living room in time to answer the door.

"Hello, Mr. Finch," James said.

"We are here to take your daughters to the movies," Alex said.

"All three?" Gloria said.

"What?" Alex said. "No, see, we…"

"My dad has three daughters," Gloria said. "Are you taking all of us?"

"What?" James said. "No, see, I don't…"

"Gloria, go tell your sisters their dates are here," Rollie said.

"Don't go away, boys," Gloria said as she scooted off to the bedrooms.

"Why would we go away?" Alex said.

"Come in," Rollie said.

James and Alex followed Rollie to the living room where Gloria reappeared. "Now, where were we?" she said. "I hope it's a movie I like."

"What? No, see we're…" James said.

Grace and Giselle entered the living room.

"Saved by the bell," Gloria said.

"What bell?" Grace said.

"Eleven o'clock, remember," Rollie said.

"We know," Grace said.

As James opened the door, he said, "What bell?"

"Never mind," Grace said.

Gloria went to the window and looked out. "Boy, are they stupid," she said.

"So," Rollie said. "Where should we go for dinner?"

•   •   •

Gloria chose Italian and Rollie took her to the Roma on Queens Boulevard. Gloria ordered spaghetti with meatballs, while Rollie went with lasagna. Both came with salad and garlic rolls.

"I'm glad we're alone, because there's something I want to discuss with you," Rollie said.

"Uh oh," Gloria said.

"Never mind uh oh," Rollie said. "I spoke to your teacher after your last report card."

"I got straight B plus," Gloria said.

"I know," Rollie said. "And your teacher thinks you're not even trying. She said you could be straight-A-plus across the board if you wanted to."

Gloria looked down for a moment.

"It's embarrassing, Dad," she said.

"What is?" Rollie said.

"The smart ones are labeled nerds," Gloria said.

"The smart ones get ahead in life while those calling the smart ones nerds work at fast food restaurants," Rollie said. "Don't hide your potential because of peer pressure. Next year you start high school. You want to go into high school at your best. Understand?"

Gloria nodded. "I understand."

"Good. What should we get for dessert?" Rollie asked.

CHAPTER TWENTY-NINE

"We weren't expecting you on Monday, Rollie," Schram said.

"I had to come into the city anyway," Rollie said. "I figured I might as well pick up the witness list."

"We appreciate that, Rollie," Gitter said.

"And don't be shy on the billing hours, Marks is a billionaire," Schram said.

"Something I wanted to talk to you about," Rollie said. "When you were researching the tontine bylaws, what does it say would happen if Rose dies before the last member? Who takes over to administer the funds?"

"In the death of Rose Senior, the baton was passed to Rose Junior," Gitter said.

"In other words, nobody," Schram said. "Rose Junior hasn't designated his replacement as yet."

"Which means?" Rollie said.

"The sole survivor would have to find a probate lawyer and basically start over to release the funds," Schram said.

"That could take some time," Gitter said. "If the sole survivor died before that happened, the money could wind up belonging to the government."

"I'm going to see Rose next, I'll mention it to him," Rollie said.

"Let us know what you want to do with the witness list," Gitter said.

• • •

"Mr. Finch, I wasn't expecting you," Rose said as Rollie entered Rose's office.

"I'm on the way to visit Enache," Rollie said. "I thought if you weren't tied up you could join me."

Rose glanced at the clock on his desk. "I suppose I could finish this will later."

"Good," Rollie said.

• • •

As Rollie drove across the Brooklyn Bridge, he said, "Mr. Rose, has it ever occurred to you that you might be in danger?"

"Me? Danger. What for?" Rose said.

"The same reason the six disappeared," Rollie said. "The money at the end of the rainbow."

"You don't really believe that," Rose said. "Do you?"

"Unfortunately, I do," Rollie said. "Do you own a gun?"

"Twenty years or so ago I purchased a Smith & Wesson Model 60 revolver to keep in my bedroom," Rose said. "It's in the closet somewhere."

"That's a fine gun for the nightstand, but you need something smaller for personal defense," Rollie said. "Do you have a carry permit?"

"I do," Rose said.

"We'll stop at the gun store in Yonkers later," Rollie said. "Pick up something small and light you can carry around."

"Maybe I should," Rose said.

"There's something else, too," Rollie said. "In researching the tontine bylaws Gitter and Schram discovered that you haven't appointed a successor to yourself in case something happens to you before the funds are released."

"I… I don't know who to appoint," Rose said. "I don't make friends easily you know. I've kept to myself most of my life."

"But you know other attorneys?" Rollie said.

"I'm sure you know other private investigators," Rose said. "Would you feel comfortable asking them to take responsibility of one of your cases in the event you died?"

"Honestly, no," Rollie said. "But Gitter and Schram would do it for you out of respect for your father."

"I suppose I could ask them," Rose said.

Rollie grinned. "I think they're expecting your call," he said.

Rose nodded. "Let me ask you this. As a retired homicide detective and private investigator, do you really believe my life is in danger?"

"Until we know who is behind the missing six and why, I would have to say yes," Rollie said.

"I can't wait to be done with this," Rose said.

"I'm sure Enache feels the same way," Rollie said.

"Let me ask you," Rose said. "All I know are wills and estates, so forgive me my lack of understanding of the criminal mind. Who and how does someone get their hands on the $12,000,000?"

Across the bridge and into Brooklyn, Rollie said, "Several ways actually. There could be a seventh man involved. He disappeared deliberately and then got rid of the missing six. Before he could get to Enache, we got to Enache first. That is the reason I brought in Redford."

"That would leave a serial killer wandering around," Rose said.

"It would," Rollie said. "Another way is it's an inside job."

"Inside how?" Rose said.

"Enache hired somebody to eliminate his competition leaving him king of the hill," Rollie said.

"The man is eighty-six and can't walk ten paces without stopping to rest," Rose said.

"Which doesn't prevent him from bringing in a partner for a piece of the pie, a partner willing to do the dirty work," Rollie said.

"Do you really believe that?" Rose said as Rollie parked curbside outside Enache's townhouse.

"It doesn't matter what I believe," Rollie said. "It only matters what can be proved. Let's go."

.   .   .

Enache and one of Redford's men were playing chess at the coffee table in the living room when Rose and Rollie entered.

"And you are?" Rollie said.

"Name is Mike Thomas, Mr. Finch," Thomas said. "Paul said to expect your call. He didn't mention you'd be stopping by."

"Where is he?" Rollie said.

"He took my granddaughter to the market," Enache said. "They left about an hour ago."

"Want me to call him?" Thomas said.

"No, we'll wait," Rollie said.

"Let's finish the game," Enache said.

Twenty minutes later, Abbey and Redford returned with several bags of groceries.

"Rollie, why didn't you tell me you were coming," Redford said.

"Last minute decision," Rollie said. "We need to talk."

Rollie, Redford, and Rose went into the den, leaving Enache with Thomas.

"Just an alert," Rollie said. "I'm looking into the possibility of a seventh man still alive in the tontine that might have eliminated the other six. In which case he'll be looking to make it seven."

"A seventh man?" Redford said. "Who?"

"I'm running down the list of names," Rollie said. "I should know in a few days. In the meantime, no guests of any kind, even if Abbey and Enache know them."

"No problem," Redford said. "I don't think the girl has any friends anyway. Her whole life seems to be taking care of the old man."

"Keep him ticking for another twenty-five days," Rollie said.

"Actually, the paperwork to release the funds will take several days," Rose said.

"Make that thirty days," Rollie said.

"They want him they got to go through me and my men," Redford said.

"They'll be a bonus at the end of this," Rose said.

"We'll earn it," Redford said.

There was a knock on the door to the den. It opened and Abbey stepped inside. "Do you want to stay for lunch?" she said.

Rollie looked at Finch. "Why not?" Rollie said.

•   •   •

"She is a very good cook," Rose said.

"She is," Rollie admitted. "Redford better watch himself or he'll gain ten pounds before the assignment is over."

Rollie took the Henry Hudson Parkway to the Saw Mill River Parkway to Yonkers Avenue.

"We're almost there," Rollie said. "Do you have your permit?"

"In my wallet," Rose said. "I have to admit I'm a bit nervous about this."

"You already own a gun," Rollie said.

"Not to carry around," Rose said. "In case someone broke in I'd be able to protect myself. I haven't picked it up in years."

"Make sure it's loaded," Rollie said. "What we're looking for today is for personal protection."

Rollie pulled into the parking lot of a large Yonkers gun store and range. "I shoot here sometimes," he said.

Rose nodded.

"Relax, it's not a big deal," Rollie said.

Rose nodded again.

Rose followed Rollie into the gun store where several people were browsing at the counter.

"Mr. Finch, I haven't seen you in months," a man behind the counter said.

"Too much work and very little play," Rollie said. "Todd, this is John Rose, a lawyer from Manhattan. We're interested in something small and light he can carry with him."

"I think I got what you need," Todd said.

Todd showed Rollie and Rose a Beretta model 21 pistol. "Small, light and holds seven rounds of .22 Long Colt ammunition."

Rollie inspected the .21 and handed it to Rose.

"It's so light," Rose said.

"But accurate, reliable and very easy to conceal and carry," Todd said. "It's very popular with men and women with…"

"Small hands," Rose said.

Todd nodded.

"What do you think, Rollie," Rose said.

"I think it's exactly what you're looking for," Rollie said.

"I'll get the paperwork started and then you can try it out at our range," Todd said.

.　　.　　.

"You did well," Rollie said.

"I fired thirty-five bullets and only hit the bull's eye six times," Rose said.

"From twenty-one feet," Rollie said. "An attacker is going to be much closer than that."

Rollie pulled curbside in front of Rose's building. "I'll call you tomorrow with any updates," Rollie said.

"Thank you, Rollie, for everything," Rose said.

Rollie nodded. "Keep that little gun handy," he said.

.　　.　　.

"This seventh man theory of yours may be right, but we've checked fifty-five names so far and every one of them is dead according to Social Security," Teal said.

"When do you think you'll finish?" Rollie said.

"Wednesday."

"Bring the results in exchange for dinner," Rollie said. "I'll have the girls make fried chicken with mashed potatoes and chocolate cake for dessert."

"Heartless, Rollie," Teal said. "You're heartless."

"Seven thirty," Rollie said.

CHAPTER THIRTY

Rollie found Gloria and Mrs. Kravitz in the kitchen, preparing dinner.

"Smells good," Rollie said.

"Baked ziti," Gloria said.

"Your sisters will be home by seven," Rollie said. "Mrs. Kravitz, will you join us?"

"Please," Gloria said.

"Well, alright," Mrs. Kravitz said.

"Good. I'll be in the office for a bit," Rollie said.

Buddy was in the cat bed with mama cat and the kittens. Mama cat was giving Buddy a bath with some serious licking.

"Can Armageddon be far behind," Rollie said as he took his chair.

He opened his notebook, picked up his pen and stared at the clean sheet of paper.

Then he made some notes on the day's activities. He wanted to spend the day with Rose to access his frame of mind. The diminutive lawyer was more like a timid rabbit than a man who could plot a complicated scheme to get his hands on twelve million dollars.

But Rollie had worked several cases before where the least likely suspect turned out to be the guilty party.

Eleven years ago, he worked a homicide case in Manhattan. A wealthy stockbroker was found murdered in his West Side

Townhouse. The man had dozens of enemies. Suspects included clients who went broke on his advice, two ex-wives, three mistresses and two ex business partners, all with axes to grind.

The murderer turned out to be the doorman of the building who, after being snubbed for a Christmas tip five consecutive years, snapped and shot the businessman dead one dark night in January.

Could Rose be that frustrated doorman? A diminutive, invisible lawyer who prepared wills and estates for wealthy elites without ever so much as a dipping his little toe into their pond.

Did he have the raw courage and nerves to pull off such a scheme? He would need a partner on the inside.

A seventh man.

Or.

Enache.

Who else besides Rose knew where all the members of the tontine were located?

If Rose killed Enache, he would have to hold onto the funds for a decade before making a million in interest. He would be seventy-one by that time, if he made it.

But if he made a deal with Enache to have the missing six killed in exchange for say two million, he would collect now while still young enough to enjoy it.

Rollie set his pen down when Joanna called on the hard-line phone.

"I'm glad you called, I was giving myself a headache," Rollie said.

"That tontine thing?"

"Yeah."

"Well, I'll be there in one week, so I hope you don't plan on working," Joanna said.

"Nope."

"Will it be resolved by then?"

"No, but don't worry about it, I'm entitled to the holidays," Rollie said.

"Good. Rollie, I miss you. A lot," Joanna said. "Is it wrong of me to say that?"

"Nope and it's something we need to talk about when you get here," Rollie said.

They chatted for a bit and then Rollie typed his notes into a document in his computer.

To Rollie's surprise, Rose called him on the cell phone.

"Mr. Rose, is something wrong?" Rollie said.

"No, but I've been thinking," Rose said. "You've really gone above and beyond what you were hired to do. I hope you've been keeping accurate records of your time and expenses."

"I have," Rollie said.

"Do you think you can get me in to see Gitter and Schram tomorrow?" Rose said. "I'd like to ask them if they would agree to assume responsibility for the Tontine in case something happens to me."

"Has something happened?" Rollie said.

"Just a dose of common sense," Rose said.

"I'll call you tomorrow morning," Rollie said.

"Thank you," Rose said. "Goodnight."

If Rose masterminded this scheme, he was the world's greatest actor. Or such a sociopath he could fool a polygraph test.

Or both.

Or none.

Maybe Rose was exactly what he appeared to be, a timid, little man treading water as he went through life.

Rollie looked at the clock on his desk. Grace and Giselle would be home in an hour.

He opened Gitter and Schram's file of witnesses for the Marks trial. A waiter at a restaurant witnessed Marks and his wife arguing during dinner. Construction workers at a job site witnessed Marks yelling at his wife when she visited him at the site. A doorman at Marks's building witnessed Marks and Justine arguing when he opened a limo door for them.

A dozen others witnessed Marks and Justine arguing in public.

The doorman on duty that day stated that no stranger entered the building all day and Marks came home alone at 6:30 in the evening.

No one can say that Marks ever put a hand on his wife.

The average person might say, big deal, everybody argues.

A prosecutor in court will stress the point that the marriage was bad and Marks was found with his wife's blood on his hand and knee, and his fingerprints on the knife.

Damning in court before a jury of twelve that probably hated the wealthy to begin with.

Rollie made some notes for tomorrow and then went to the kitchen to check on Gloria and Mrs. Kravitz.

Grace and Giselle would be home in fifteen. "We have time to take Buddy for a walk," Rollie said.

"I'll grab my jacket and the leash," Gloria said.

Buddy tugged and sniffed his way around the block while Gloria held the leash.

"Dad, I hate to say this but the cat belongs to Buddy now," Gloria said.

"I know," Rollie said. "Once the kittens are gone, the cat is all his."

"We need to name her," Gloria said.

"You three talk about it," Rollie said. "You'll come up with something."

When the reached home, Grace's car was in the driveway.

"Good, they're home," Grace said. "I'm starving."

•   •   •

After the dishes were done and Grace and Giselle tackled their homework, Gloria and Rollie walked Mrs. Kravitz home.

"Dad, mind if I spend some time with Buddy and the cat?" Gloria said.

"I don't see why not," Rollie said.

They took Buddy back to the garage where the cat was stretching her legs outside the bed. Buddy greeted the cat with a sniff and a lick and then he got into the bed to snuggle with the kittens while the cat ate from her food bowl.

Gloria sat beside the cat bed and petted the kittens.

Rollie went to his desk and read through the Marks witness list again. There was no way to refute the witnesses' testimony about the public arguments.

And the prosecutor will drum it into the jury's heads about the knife, blood, and fingerprints.

"Hey, Dad, look," Gloria said.

Rollie turned around. Gloria was sitting in the yoga position with the cat on her lap. The cat rubbed against Gloria as she petted her.

Rollie closed the file and went to sit beside Gloria. He reached out and stroked the cat behind the neck.

"I guess she's ours now," he said.

CHAPTER THIRTY-ONE

"We'd be happy to assume responsibility in case something happened to you before the funds are released," Gitter said.

"Not that I expect something to happen to me, but one never knows about these things and I would not like to see Mr. Enache get cheated," Rose said.

"He won't," Schram said. "Now, is there something we don't know about?"

"That's my fault," Rollie said. "I explained to Mr. Rose my theory on a seventh man and made him a little nervous."

"How is everything going with Mr. Enache?" Gitter said.

"Quiet for the moment," Rollie said.

"I doubt very much you're in any danger, Mr. Rose," Schram said.

"Even so, thank you," Rose said.

"I need to talk to Mr. Gitter and Schram on another matter," Rollie said.

"I'll take a cab back to the office," Rose said.

After Rose left the office, Rollie said, "I've been reading the witness list. I can see where the DA is going with this. One after the other to establish Marks and his wife fought a lot and then put on display to the jury the knife and bloody hand and knee and let them draw their own conclusions."

"We've been prepping him for the stand, but we need more if

we're going to win this one," Gitter said.

"I would like to see Marks again and also get me what you can on his wife Justine," Rollie said. "Her spending habits, friends, hobbies, anything and everything."

"We already have most of that," Schram said.

"I'll take what you have," Rollie said.

"We'll set up Marks for Friday," Gitter said. "His penthouse is off limits as a crime scene, so he's staying at one of his hotels."

"Call me Thursday with a time," Rollie said.

.   .   .

On the way home, Rollie stopped at the grocery store on Queens Boulevard and picked up ten plump chicken breasts and legs and whatever else he'd need to make fried chicken.

Gloria and Mrs. Kravitz were in the kitchen where Gloria was doing her homework.

"I'll be done in a little while," Gloria said.

"Good. We'll take Buddy for a walk and then start dinner for Uncle Bill," Rollie said.

"Is that the nice-looking gentleman I see sometimes?" Mrs. Kravitz said.

"My partner from when I was a detective," Rollie said.

"Does he like chocolate cake?" Mrs. Kravitz said.

"Very much," Rollie said.

"Do you mind if I bake one? I was going to anyway," Mrs. Kravitz said.

"I know Bill won't mind at all," Rollie said.

"Then I'll be back," Mrs. Kravitz said.

Rollie went to his office, sat at his desk, and opened the file on Justine Marks. Before she married Marks, she was Justine Claus and she worked for the Marks Organization in marketing. She made $80,000 a year and lived in a small apartment on the West Side.

Her parents live in Jersey and she has one younger brother who is a Jersey State Trooper.

Marks was coming off his third divorce when he spotted Justine at a grand opening of one of his hotels in Atlantic City. After a whirlwind courtship, they were married at one of his country clubs in Florida.

Rollie flipped through documentation on her spending. She used Marks like a cash machine. She was spending $50,000 a month on hair, makeup and clothes. She belonged to a gym on 5th Avenue where the dues were $2,000 a month. She had regular visits to an exclusive spa that cost $10,000 a month.

Rollie paused for a moment. What could possibly cost $10,000 a month at a spa?

Justine also had a personal trainer that visited the penthouse several times a week.

Marks occupied the twenty-four-room penthouse apartment. However, everybody in the building was a billionaire or close to it. A bottom floor apartment would set you back $12,000. Anything above the tenth floor started at $25,000,000.

Rollie couldn't imagine the world these people lived in, but one thing was for certain, she wasn't killed for money.

What could cause a man like Marks to fly into such a rage that he killed his wife in a fit of anger?

Jealousy.

He wanted more kids. She wanted wealth. If he divorced her, prenup or not, she would cost a quarter of a billion to get rid of.

Would a man worth 300 times that amount kill over it?

Probably not.

Would he kill over jealousy?

Possibly.

If he walked in on her while in bed with a lover, it might be enough to put him over the edge, but that didn't happen and there were no signs she had a lover.

The possibilities of what happened were endless.

"Hey, Dad, I'm ready," Gloria said as she entered the office.

"Grab your coat, I'll get the leash," Rollie said.

.   .   .

When they returned from walking Buddy, Rollie and Gloria seasoned the chicken and got it ready to fry.

Gloria took care of the mashed potatoes while Rollie fried up the chicken in the air fryer. Gloria then went to Mrs. Kravitz to pick up the chocolate cake.

By the time Grace and Giselle got home from the store, dinner was nearly ready.

Teal arrived at 7:30 and set his briefcase on the sofa. "My mouth is watering," he said as he sniffed the kitchen.

Talk at the table was light and airy with stories about the pet store, Buddy, the cat and the kittens.

"You'll need a cat bed, bowls for food and water, toys, brushes and a carrier," Grace said. "And a vet of course."

"Of course," Teal said.

"We'll bring you coffee and cake," Grace said.

Rollie and Teal went to the office. Teal set his briefcase on the desk and picked up one of his kittens, then sat in the chair.

"So, what do you got for me?" Rollie said.

"Your instincts were right as usual," Teal said.

"You mean there is a seventh man?" Rollie said.

"A sixty-three-year-old ski instructor living in Vermont," Teal said. "I'll let you read the details, but the short of it is his parents invested in the tontine and passed it on to him when they died thirty years ago. So, his name shows up on the list of one hundred."

"A sixty-three-year-old ski instructor is not too old to go around killing off his competition," Rollie said.

"No, he is not," Teal said.

Grace, Giselle and Gloria entered the office. "We brought you coffee and chocolate cake," Grace said and set the tray on the desk.

"Thank you, girls," Teal said. "You saved me from a dinner of carrot sticks, lettuce leave and hummus."

"What's hummus?" Gloria said.

"Something that looks like it came out of a baby diaper," Teal said.

"Gross," Gloria said.

"We have to finish the dishes," Grace said.

Rollie and Teal ate their cake and coffee at the desk.

"So, what do you plan to do," Teal said.

"Check out the ski instructor," Rollie said.

"Want me to go along?" Teal said.

"I could use the company if you can get clearance," Rollie said.

"Call me tomorrow," Teal said.

"I'll do better than that, I'll take you to lunch," Rollie said.

"Now you are talking," Teal said.

"I'll walk you out so you can say goodbye to the girls," Rollie said.

•　　•　　•

Alex Funar turned sixty-five two months ago. His parents came to America as children to escape the Nazis and settled in Manhattan. They met, married and had Alex in the mid fifties.

They were not city people and looked to relocate to the country where they could enjoy skiing in the winter and they settled on Vermont. Before leaving New York, they invested in the tontine.

In Vermont, they invested in a small ski lodge and worked for years to build it up and make it successful.

Alex learned to ski by the time he was two and was competing by the time he was ten. The ski lodge grew in stature and when Alex was eighteen, he was selected as an alternative on the American Olympic Ski Team.

A knee injury prevented him from competing, but not from acting as head instructor for the lodge. When Alex was twenty-six, his parents died in a car accident, leaving him as sole owner of the lodge. Alex had a young wife, who died with his parents in the accident. He never remarried.

His parents will transferred their tontine investment to Alex and it was recorded by Rose's father, John Sr.

After Kohn Sr. died and left the business to his son, John Rose Jr., the name Alex Funar got lost with his parents in the list of deceased tontine members.

At age sixty-three, Alex was certainly the front runner for the twelve million.

Rollie closed the file, said goodnight to Buddy and the cat and decided to turn in early because tomorrow was going to be a long day.

CHAPTER THIRTY-TWO

Rose read Teal's police report on Alex Funar and his face drained of all color.

Rollie got some water from the water cooler and gave the paper cup to Rose.

"Thank you," Rose said as he sipped water.

"You need to tell Enache," Rollie said.

"Yes, of course," Rose said.

"I'll drive," Rollie said.

. . .

"How did you locate Mr. Funar?" Rose said.

"I requested a search of Social Security checks being delivered to any names on the list beside Enache," Rollie said. "Funar's name popped up as he recently applied before he turned sixty-five."

"Very smart of you," Rose said. He wiped his brow with a handkerchief. "Oh, how do I break the news to Mr. Enache?"

"I'll do it if you'd like," Rollie said.

"No, it's my duty," Rose said. "But I could use your help if I flounder. I'm not particularly good at these things."

"I doubt something like this has come up before," Rollie said.

"No, I suppose not," Rose said. "What a mess."

Rollie parked in front of Enache's townhouse.
"Let's try to clean it up," Rollie said.

•   •   •

"The old man is asleep," Redford said. "He didn't feel well at breakfast and Abbey gave him a sedative."
"Oh dear," Rose said.
"Why, what's the matter?" Redford said. "It's as quiet as a church around here."
"Where is Abigail?" Rollie said.
"In the study," Redford said. "She said she had some bills to pay. What's going on, Rollie?"
"We need to speak to her," Rollie said.
Redford led Rose and Rollie to the study where Abbey was behind a desk. "Mr. Rose, Mr. Finch, I wasn't expecting you," she said.
"I'm afraid we have some news," Rollie said.
Rollie did most of the talking, telling Abbey about Funar in Vermont.
"My grandfather will be very disappointed," she said.
"Actually, maybe it would be best you didn't mention this to him until after we check this out thoroughly," Rollie said. "No sense giving him a shock unless Mr. Funar really is next in line."
"In hindsight, I agree," Rose said.
"Alright, I won't mention this to him," Abbey said.
"Wait for us to return," Rollie said. "We'll tell him."
Abbey nodded. "Alright," she said.

•   •   •

"Did we do the right thing?" Rose said.

"I think so," Rollie said. "No sense giving Enache a stroke if Funar doesn't turn out to be ahead of Enache."

"But he's twenty plus years younger," Rose said. "Enache couldn't possibly outlive him."

"That's not what I mean," Rollie said. "Over the next few days, search for anything that might eliminate Funar. A clause that says the tontine can't be passed down to a relative. Something like that. If it's in there, find it. If it isn't there, Funar will just have to wait for Enache to die."

"Maybe Gitter and Schram can assist me with research?" Rose said.

"I have a meeting with them tomorrow, I'll ask them," Rollie said.

"Thank you," Rose said. "You've been an enormous help with this entire mess."

"That's why you hired me," Rollie said.

.   .   .

Teal smacked his lips before biting into a double-bacon cheeseburger. "I have to admit, Rollie, that you have a flare for complicating things."

"It's my fault that Funar is still alive?" Rollie said.

"You could have let the sleeping dog sleep," Teal said.

"Sleeping dogs don't catch murderers," Rollie said. "Somebody knows who killed the missing six, Bill."

"And Funar automatically is a suspect because?" Teal said.

"He's in his early sixties. A lifelong skier and athlete," Rollie said. "He knows all about the tontine from his parents. He takes his time to plot things out right and gets rid of the missing six, leaving just Enache. Enache is eighty-six. Funar can afford to wait for Enache to die and claim the prize, once Funar lets it be known he's still around."

Teal nodded as he took another bite of his burger. "Like I said, you have a way of stirring things up," he said.

"I'm going to Vermont on Monday, are you going?" Rollie said.

"I could use some maple syrup," Teal said.

CHAPTER THIRTY-THREE

Rollie sat at his desk and stared at the blank page in his notebook. He sipped coffee from his favorite mug. With the office door closed, the only noise came from the heating vent. Behind him the cat, kittens and Buddy were asleep in the cat bed.

He picked up his pen and started to make notes. Each member of the tontine had a complete list of all the other members. When Funar's parents died, he inherited their place on the tontine and the list of names. Fast-forward forty years and Funar knows he is high on the list to inherit and decides to take matters into his own hands and he eliminates the missing six. He knows Enache is eighty-six and the last one, besides himself, on the list of one hundred.

Funar is left with two options. *Kill Enache and claim the prize. Wait for Enache to die of natural causes and then step forward and claim the prize as the sole surviving member of the tontine.*

Option A was quicker given the exceptional care Enache received. Enache could live another two, even three years.

Option B was slower, but safer in that his low profile kept the risk of being a suspect to a minimum.

Rollie sat back and thought about Funar's options for a while. It was true that Funar was more than twenty years younger than Enache, but Rollie had no way of knowing his health record. He could be on death's door, for all he knew.

There was a third scenario. *Funar had forgotten about the tontine and went about his daily life of running his ski lodge and was blissfully ignorant of Enache, the missing six and the twelve million dollars.*

All three were plausible.

However, option C meant another party was involved. Someone else removed the missing six and was waiting in the wings to take out Enache and claim the prize. Even Enache himself with a little help could be behind all of it.

Rollie typed his notes into a document in his computer, and then went to change into sweats. He returned to the office and did thirty minutes on the step climber and another thirty on the Bowflex.

Money wasn't the root of all evil, but the pursuit of it certainly was.

After a quick shower and change of clothes, Rollie found the girls doing their homework in the kitchen. Each of his daughters had a laptop computer and was entering their homework online.

Gone were the days of pencils, paper, erasers, and penmanship.

"Gloria, almost done?" he said.

"Two minutes," Gloria said.

"When you're done, we'll take Buddy for his walk," Rollie said.

•   •   •

"So, we've been trying to pick a name for the cat," Gloria said as she and Rollie walked Buddy around the block.

"And?" Rollie said.

"Well, Grace likes Fluffy, which doesn't make sense since the cat is short haired," Gloria said. "Giselle likes Lucky, since it was luck that brought her to us."

"And you?" Rollie said.

"I don't know what to call the mama cat," Gloria said.

"What's wrong with that?" Rollie said.

"What? Mama Cat?" Gloria said.

"That's what she is," Rollie said.

"Huh. I'll see what Grace and Giselle think," Gloria said.

"What should we have for dinner tonight?" Rollie asked.

CHAPTER THIRTY-FOUR

As they entered the lobby of one of Marks's hotels on 42nd and Park Avenue, Schram said, "Ask Rose to stop by the office and we'll see what we can do with his research."

"I'll tell him," Rollie said.

They stopped by the desk and were given clearance for the penthouse elevator.

"According to what you gave me, Justine Marks spent money like a drunken sailor on shore leave," Rollie said.

They entered the private, penthouse elevator and rode to the top.

"By our standards," Schram said. "To Marks, he would barely notice. I doubt paying her two hundred and fifty mil to divorce her would hardly be an inconvenience."

"So why kill her?" Rollie said. "Homicide 101, the killer needs a motive to kill."

"That's pretty good, Rollie," Gitter said. "We'll use that line in court."

The elevator opened directly to the penthouse suite of eight rooms. Dressed casually in jeans and a pullover shirt, with running shoes on his feet, Marks greeted them as they stepped out of the elevator car.

"Glad you could make it," Marks said. "Something to drink?"

"Coffee would be good," Schram said.

"Come to the kitchen," Marks said.

The kitchen was twice the size of Rollie's and gleaming with brass and marble. On one of the counters was a brass espresso machine. Five thousand a night bought a lot of perks.

"Have a seat, this will only take a minute," Marks said.

Rollie, Schram and Gitter took chairs at a highly polished dining table. Within the allotted minute, Marks brought four cups of espresso to the table, and then sat beside Gitter.

Rollie sampled the espresso. It was excellent.

"Alright, let's get to this," Marks said.

"This is not a joke, Mr. Marks," Rollie said. "If I was still in homicide and this was my case, I'd be working my ass off to put you away for life."

Marks glared at Rollie. "It's bad enough I have to take shit from the media, I won't from people I hire," he said.

"You didn't hire me, Gitter and Schram did," Rollie said. "And as far as I'm concerned, you're too rich for your own damn good."

Marks jumped to his feet. "Get out," he said. "Get the fuck out before I throw you out."

"Right again, Rollie," Gitter said.

"Right about what?" Marks said.

"That your alpha male personality wouldn't hold up on the stand," Schram said.

"The lead prosecutor would have you for lunch and dessert," Gitter said.

Marks slumped into his chair.

"We have time to work with you," Schram said. "We're hiring a coach to take you through the process."

Marks looked at Rollie. "I guess I flew off the handle," he said.

"Here's how it's going to go," Rollie said. "When did you first plan to kill your wife? Was it after you saw how she spent money like water or when she told you no children?"

"What?" Marks said. "I didn't kill—"

"Answer the question, Mr. Marks," Rollie said.

"I didn't plan to—" Marks said.

"Your honor, permission to treat the witness as hostile," Rollie said.

"Hostile? You won't let me get a fucking word in edgewise," Marks said.

"Mr. Marks, we're trying to save you from life in prison, not help you design a building," Rollie said.

"Yes, you're right of course," Marks said. "To answer your question, I never planned to kill my wife, nor did I kill her. As for her spending habits, she was on an allowance of sixty thousand a month. How and when she spent it was her business."

"Better," Rollie said. "With a proper coach and enough time, you'll do fine on the stand."

"I hope so," Marks said.

"So, let me ask you this," Rollie said. "Was Justine having an affair?"

"An affair?" Marks said. "No, she was not."

"How many hours do you work in a week?" Rollie said.

"Sixty, seventy, I don't keep track," Marks said.

"Out by seven, home by nine, how do you know she wasn't having an affair?" Rollie said.

Marks looked at Rollie.

"It's going to come up in court," Rollie said. "It's best we put it on the table now."

"I suspected," Marks said. "I had no proof of anything, but a man suspects when his wife is stepping out."

"Did you confront her about it?" Rollie said.

"No. Maybe I should have, but I didn't," Marks said.

"Any suspicions who?" Rollie said.

"No, none," Marks said. "I did question the doormen. After all, they do work for me. I checked all sign-in sheets and spoke to every security person in the building. There was nothing. No visitors during the day except for her female yoga instructor."

"I'm going to poke around your building a bit, okay with you?" Rollie said.

Marks nodded. "I built and own the damn thing and I can't even set foot inside my own apartment," he said.

"Thanks for the time, Mr. Marks," Rollie said. "I'll be in touch soon."

•   •   •

On Park Avenue, Rollie hailed a cab and rode with Gitter and Schram to their office a half mile south.

"What are you thinking, Rollie?" Gitter said.

"I'll let you know when I figure things out," Rollie said. "In the meantime, I'll stop by Rose's office and tell him to give you a call."

When the cab arrived at Gitter and Schram's office, Rollie left them on the sidewalk and walked to the lot where he parked his car.

He drove to Rose's office on 8th Avenue and found a parking space on the street.

Rose was working on a pile of documents when Rollie entered his office.

"Estates are the worst," Rose said. "Especially when multiple family members are involved."

"I just left Gitter and Schram," Rollie said. "Give them a call. They'll help you out as best they can."

"I can't thank you enough," Rose said. "I'm exhausted from all this."

"Hopefully, it will be over soon and you can take a vacation," Rollie said.

"I was thinking that very thing," Rose said. "You know I own a cottage on Lake Winnipesauke in New Hampshire. That's near the White Mountains. A few days in the country might do me some good."

"Sounds like a good idea," Rollie said.

"Maybe your family would like a day in the country?" Rose said. "It's quite beautiful at Christmas time."

"Sounds good," Rollie said. "Oh, by the way, I'll be going to Vermont on Monday to talk to Funar."

"Want me to go with you?" Rose said.

"Not necessary, but I'll call you afterward," Rollie said.

"I guess I better call Gitter and Schram," Rose said.

. . .

Rollie brought two containers of coffee into Teal's office and set them on the desk. "I have a proposal," Rollie said.

"No donuts?" Teal said.

"Too late in the day. I didn't want to spoil your appetite for dinner," Rollie said.

"What appetite? Who is hungry for lettuce leaves and carrot sticks?" Teal said.

"Rabbits. Now will you shut up and listen," Rollie said. "It's three hundred miles to Vermont to Funar's ski lodge. I'd like to leave Sunday afternoon and stay overnight, so we can talk to him on Monday and be back early Monday evening."

"Sunday night, huh?" Teal said.

"Think of the real dinner, breakfast and lunch we'd have instead of bunny food," Rollie said.

"What time do we leave?" Teal said.

•   •   •

At dinner, Rollie told the girls his plans for Sunday. "Grace, you're eighteen now and I trust your judgment, so I won't ask Mrs. Kravitz to stay over while I'm in Vermont. I expect you to make sure things go smoothly around here until I get home."

"Don't worry, Dad, we'll be okay," Grace said.

"It also means up and to school on time," Rollie said.

"We know," Giselle said.

From the garage, Buddy started barking.

"Something must be wrong," Gloria said.

They went to the garage and found Buddy barking at the kittens who had climbed out of the bed. Mama cat was frantically trying to pick them up and return them to the bed, but the kittens didn't want to go.

"Girls, give them a hand," Rollie said. "And something like that better not happen here while I'm away."

CHAPTER THIRTY-FIVE

Teal checked his cell phone as Rollie drove north on Interstate 95.

"Do you know they have snow in the mountains in Vermont already?" Teal said.

"That's why the lodges are already open for business," Rollie said.

"What's the name of this mountain we're going to?" Teal said.

"Killington," Rollie said. "It's in the Green Mountains."

"I skipped breakfast so we could stop in Albany for lunch at that Mexican steakhouse," Teal said.

"You're the only cop I know who could be bought with a hamburger," Rollie said. "Did you check Funar's finances?"

"His lodge does about $800,000 for the ski season," Teal said. "After payroll and expenses, he keeps about $80,000 for himself. He closes it in May and reopens in November. He draws about $2,000 a month from Social Security. Nothing shady at all in his business or his lifestyle. He even lives in a small apartment in the lodge."

"And him personally?" Rollie said.

"He never remarried, has no warrants or arrests on his record," Teal said.

"None of which eliminates him as a suspect," Rollie said.

"The Son of Sam was a postal clerk and Dahmer was an all-American boy," Teal said.

Rollie took the exit for Albany.

"Lunch," Teal said.

.   .   .

Rollie and Teal left their ski parkas in the car as it was fifty-five degrees in Albany. They ordered steaks at the Mexican steakhouse and discussed the various theories concerning the tontine.

"Funar is certainly young and strong enough to kill six old people for twelve million," Teal said.

"But not alone," Rollie said. "Remember, he was too young at the time the tontine was founded. He was willed his place after his parents died. He didn't know anybody on the list or where they lived."

"Only this Rose character had that information," Teal said.

Rollie nodded.

"Rose and Funar worked together to eliminate the six others, hoping Enache would just die of old age," Teal said. "Or Enache and Rose worked together to eliminate the six and Funar was a surprise."

"Either way, Rose comes out not smelling like one," Rollie said.

"How long are you going to string him along?" Teal said.

"As long as it takes to get enough evidence to indict," Rollie said.

"Should we get dessert?" Teal said.

"Do you want dessert?"

"Of course, I want dessert," Teal said.

"Then we'll get dessert."

.   .   .

"Everything okay?" Rollie said.

"Fine, Dad," Gloria said. "We're taking Buddy for a walk and then we're going to make dinner."

"Is Grace handy?" Rollie said.

"Grace is a klutz," Gloria said. "Ever see her play soccer? Plus, she breaks a lot of dishes when we…"

"I meant, is she by the phone," Rollie said.

"I heard that, squirt," Grace said. "I'm here, Dad."

"Tomorrow is a school day, so Gloria goes to bed by ten," Rollie said.

"No problem, Dad."

"If I'm not back by three thirty tomorrow, Gloria stays with Mrs. Kravitz," Rollie said.

"No problem, Dad," Grace said.

"I'll talk to you later. Try not to break any dishes," Rollie said.

"Dad!"

• • •

"Vermont looks very much like upstate New York," Teal said.

"Imaginary lines," Rollie said.

"What?"

"On the map."

"Oh. Hey, how much longer to this place we're staying at?"

Rollie looked at the GPS. "Thirty minutes."

"Good. My legs are killing me from this sitting."

About thirty minutes later, Rollie pulled into the parking lot of a motel at the base of a mountain. He parked and they got out and stretched.

"Snow on the mountain, not so much on the ground," Teal said.

"This time of year, they're probably making it themselves," Rollie said. "Let's check in."

Rollie was in Room 21, Teal in 23. They met in the lobby after dropping off their luggage.

"Free coffee," Teal said as he carried two containers to a sofa by a window.

"Thanks," Rollie said.

"Quite a view," Teal said as he sat beside Rollie.

Outside the window, in the distance was the mountain. "This reminds me of when we were partners years ago," Teal said.

"I don't recall us ever going to Vermont on a case," Rollie said.

"No, but we spent a lot of time together catching bad guys," Teal said. "Do you ever miss it?"

"Sure, but my girls are my priority now," Rollie said.

"Yet, here we are, working together like it was ten years ago," Teal said.

"Except it's not ten years ago," Rollie said.

"I know I've said it before, but now I'm actually in a position to do something about it," Teal said. "As soon as I take over as Assistant Chief of Detectives, I can have you reinstated in a heartbeat."

Rollie looked at Teal.

"At least think about it," Teal said.

"This motel has a gym," Rollie said. "I'm going for a workout."

"And I'm going for a nap," Teal said.

"I'll meet you at seven for dinner," Rollie said.

●　　●　　●

From the gym, Rollie called home on his cell phone.

"Hey, Dad. Joanna called," Grace said.

"I'll call her later," Rollie said. "Everything okay on your end?"

"Fine. We're making chicken cutlets for dinner and Gloria will be in bed by ten," Grace said.

"Good," Rollie said. "I'll bring you something from Vermont."

Rollie was the only person in the gym and was able to use the lone step-climber for thirty minutes undisturbed. They gym didn't have a Bowflex, but it did have a half dozen excellent machines and Rollie utilized them for forty-five minutes.

Before he took a shower, he called Joanna in his room using his cell phone.

"I called you at home earlier," Joanna said.

"Grace told me," Rollie said.

"She said you're in Vermont with Captain Teal."

"We're working on the tontine case."

"That's what I figured," Joanna said. "The reason I called is about my flight. I'm not sure why, but I was notified it lands one hour earlier."

"More time for us," Rollie said.

Then chatted for a few minutes and then Rollie took a shower. He met Teal in the lobby at seven o'clock.

"How was your workout?" Teal said.

"Very good. How was your nap?"

"Restful," Teal said.

"Where do you want to go for dinner?" I'm sure napping worked up an appetite."

"Someplace that serves steak."

"There's a steakhouse on Route 100 not far from here," Rollie said.

•   •   •

As he sliced into a bloody rare hunk of sirloin, Teal said, "How do you want to approach this tomorrow?"

"I'll identify myself, show him my credentials and inform him of the tontine," Rollie said. "We'll gauge his reactions and go from there."

"How far is his lodge from here?" Teal said.

The other side of Killington," Rollie said. "Thirty minutes tops. We go right after breakfast."

"Whichever way this goes tomorrow, I'd like to bring Rose in for questioning," Teal said.

"I know, but let me work on him for bit longer," Rollie said. "He's the number one suspect, but we still don't know who he has doing the dirty work. I know it's not him."

"He'll spill that inside of ten minutes," Teal said.

"Sure, for a sweet deal for himself," Rollie said. "If he's our number one guy in this, I don't think we should offer up a deal to a man responsible for six murders. Do you?"

"When you put it that way, what should we get for dessert?" Teal said.

CHAPTER THIRTY-SIX

"**These pumpkin spice pancakes** are delicious," Teal said.

"Not bad at all," Rollie said.

"The bacon is cooked perfectly," Teal said. "And so is the sausage."

"I was thinking half the night about Rose," Rollie said.

"That's always been your problem, Rollie," Teal said. "You don't know when to turn it off."

"We're not here to go skiing," Rollie said.

"God forbid. So, what deep thoughts were you pontificating last night?"

"Why would Rose hire me to verify the missing six were really missing if he was behind it?" Rollie said.

"Good question. What did you come up with?"

"He's worried whoever he hired to get rid of the six might get rid of him too," Rollie said. "And he wants insurance, so he hires me knowing the man he hired would get wind of it and back off."

"You think the hired man wants a bigger cut?" Teal said.

"Or all of it," Rollie said.

"Why can't you ever take on something simple?" Teal said. "Why must your cases always be brain twisters?"

"It keeps me sharp," Rollie said. "Finish up, let's hit the road."

•   •   •

The scenery was beautiful as Rollie drove around Mount Killington. Snow covered mountain tops, pine trees and rolling hills, rustic lodges, and cabins. It could have been the backdrop for *The Sound of Music.*

Rollie turned down a dirt road that went on for two miles and ended at Funar's ski lodge.

The main building of the lodge was a large log cabin with a stone chimney. Twenty-four smaller cabins surrounded the main building in a horseshoe shape. A dozen cars were parked in the parking lot.

Three ambulances and two Vermont State Trooper cars were parked in front of the main cabin.

"Well this isn't good," Teal said.

"Maybe somebody busted a leg on the slopes?" Rollie said.

"Let's go find out," Teal said.

Rollie and Teal walked to the cabin and entered the lobby where two state troopers and six EMTs were gathered near the fireplace.

Teal showed the troopers his badge. "Captain Bill Teal, NYPD," Teal said. "We're here to see Mr. Funar."

"I'm afraid you're a day too late," a trooper said.

"What happened?" Rollie said.

"Funar, as he has done hundreds of times before, took the snow cat out after midnight to groom the trails after a fresh snow so his guests would have clean trails in the morning.

"Somehow, he managed to crash into a tree. He left the snow cat to insect the damage and the snow cat broke loose and ran him over, killing him on the spot."

"He got run over by his own snow cat?" Teal said.

"The instructors saw the cat wasn't in the garage this morning and they got worried," a trooper said. "They couldn't raise him on the radio and went up by snowmobile and found him under the cat and called us. We got a crew up there now trying to free the body."

"How does a massive machine like a snow cat run someone over?" Rollie said.

"What's your interest in Mr. Funar?" a trooper said.

"Is there someplace we can talk privately?" Rollie said.

•   •   •

Rollie, Teal and the two state troopers sat at a table in the lodge dining hall and drank coffee as they talked.

"$12,000,000 and he never even got a whiff of it," a trooper said.

"Bad timing," the other trooper said.

"Yeah, bad timing," Rollie said.

"How sure are we this was an accident?" Teal said.

"We saw it ourselves," a trooper said. "Funar was under the cat and the cat had dislodged from the tree and spilled over to its side."

"And footprints besides Funar's?" Rollie said.

"No footprints at all," a trooper said. "A half foot of new snow last night."

An EMT entered the hall. "He's down, what's left of him," he said.

•   •   •

Rollie and Teal watched the ambulance that contained Funar's body leave.

"We're writing it up as accidental death," a trooper said.

"For our files in New York, can you fax me a copy," Teal said.

"Sure thing," a trooper said. "Sorry you came all this way for nothing."

"Part of the job," Teal said.

After the troopers left, Rollie said, "Let's talk to those instructors who found him."

Hal Brook and Jake Stanton had been instructors for Funar for a dozen years. Both men were in their forties. They worked for Funar every year from November through May, and then traveled to Australia to work the winter from June to October.

"We're ski bums," Brook said. "We own nothing and nothing owns us."

"We go where the snow is and work twelve months out of the year," Stanton said.

"We been partners a long time," Brook said. "We figure to retire when we're fifty and buy our own lodge."

"How nice," Teal said.

"So, tell us what happened this morning," Rollie said.

"We left our cabins at six like we do most mornings," Brook said. "We usually check the weather in the lodge first and then get ready for the day."

"We saw the garage was open and the cat was missing," Stanton said.

"Is that unusual?" Rollie said.

"They work the cat usually from eight at night to around four in the morning grooming trails," Brook said. "It snowed last night, so they would groom until dawn and return the cat."

"Mr. Funar, he likes to run the cat himself," Stanton said. "When he wasn't back by eight, we thought something might be wrong."

"We decided to take the snowmobiles after we couldn't get him on the radio and that's when we found the cat and Mr. Funar," Brook said. "We called the police and you saw the rest."

"Is it unusual to groom the trails during a snowfall?" Rollie said.

"A heavy fall, yeah," Brook said. "A couple, three inches, Mr. Funar would do it no problem."

"Yeah, Mr. Funar knows what he's doing," Stanton said.

"Except that he crashed into a tree, got out and got run over by his own cat," Rollie said.

Brook and Stanton stared at Rollie.

"Thanks, fellows," Teal said.

After Brooks and Teal left, Rollie took out his cell phone and got the number for the Vermont weather bureau.

"Can you tell me the conditions of the snowfall last night on Mount Killington?" Rollie said.

Rollie listened for a minute and then hung up. "Two to four inches of light snow was expected," he said. "But a high wind squall blew in and caused whiteout conditions."

"He can't see and smacks into that tree," Teal said. "He gets out to check things and gravity does the rest."

"Convenient," Rollie said.

"Very."

"Come on," Rollie said.

Rollie and Teal went to the lobby of the lodge where Stanton, Brook and other employees had gathered.

"Mr. Stanton, Mr. Brook, a moment more please," Rollie said. "Outside."

Stanton and Brook followed Rollie and Teal outside the lodge.

Rollie looked at Mount Killington. "Elevation is about 4,200 feet," he said.

"About," Stanton said.

"How high up was Funar found?" Rollie asked.

"Maybe 1,500 feet," Brook said.

"Can you walk down?" Rollie said.

"Of course you can walk down, but unless you're familiar with the trails it's a risk," Stanton said.

"Funar was familiar with the trails, wasn't he?" Rollie said.

"He could walk down blindfolded," Brook said.

"So why didn't he?" Rollie said.

Brook and Stanton looked at Rollie.

"Thanks, fellows," Teal said.

Rollie stared at the mountain and rubbed his chin.

"Do not do that," Teal said.

"What?"

"Stare off into space and rub your chin," Teal said. "When you do that is when things get really fucked up."

"Let's head back," Rollie said. "We'll have lunch in Albany and have you home in time for a lettuce and carrot stick dinner."

"No hurry after lunch," Teal said.

"I want to stop for some T-shirts for the girls," Rollie said.

"And maybe some maple candy for me," Teal said.

CHAPTER THIRTY-SEVEN

"These steak fries are the size of canoes," Teal said.

Rollie took a bite of his burger and washed it down with a sip of ginger ale. "It's too much of a coincidence," he said.

"I love it when they toast the bun," Teal said.

"Doesn't it bother you that Funar has an accident right before we tell him about the tontine?" Rollie said.

"Sure does," Teal said, and ripped into his burger.

"The only other person who knew about Funar was Rose," Rollie said.

"Which doesn't prove a thing," Teal said.

"*Acta non verba*," Rollie said.

"We speak in tongues now?" Teal said.

"That's Latin. It means actions, not words," Rollie said.

"I'd love to take action except we haven't a shed of hard evidence that says Rose did anything except hire you," Teal said.

"He eliminated number seven to clear the way for Enache," Rollie said.

"Any judge I ask for an arrest warrant is going to say two words. Prove it," Teal said. "Followed by another two words. Get out."

"That scheming little son of a bitch suspected there was a seventh out there somewhere and he got me to find him for him," Rollie said.

"Can you prove it?" Teal said.

"Not one word," Rollie said.

"Action noun verbs," Teal said.

"That's *acta non*..." Rollie said.

"Never mind the Latin. Find a way to prove it and I'll arrest him," Teal said. "In the meantime, what should we get for dessert?"

•　　•　　•

Gloria and Mrs. Kravitz were baking apple fritters when Rollie arrived home.

"Hi Dad, we're making apple fritters," Gloria said.

"I can tell by the aroma," Rollie said.

"There was a minor development," Gloria said.

"Oh?"

"Look," Gloria said.

Rollie followed Gloria to her bedroom. The cat bed was in the corner of the room with the cat, Buddy and kittens tucked inside.

"Buddy kept freaking out every time the kittens tried to escape, so we figured if we locked them in my room the kittens couldn't go anywhere," Gloria said.

"I need to stretch my legs," Rollie said. "Let's take Buddy for a walk."

They returned to the kitchen with Buddy on the leash. "We won't be long," Rollie said.

"Take your time, the fritters need another fifteen minutes," Mrs. Kravitz said.

Gloria took the leash and they walked Buddy around the block.

"Joanna will be here in two days," Gloria said.

"That reminds me," Rollie said. "Her flight was changed. She gets in an hour earlier."

"Dad, we were talking and… well, are things serious with you and Joanna?" Gloria said.

"I can't answer that," Rollie said.

"We talked about it and…" Gloria said.

"I can't answer that because we haven't talked about it," Rollie said. "If and when we do talk about it, you three will be the first to know. Okay?"

"Okay," Gloria said.

"What were you planning for dinner?" Rollie said.

"Mrs. Kravitz has lasagna in her oven since we're making fritters in ours," Gloria said.

"I hope she's staying to help eat it," Rollie said.

• • •

Accident or murder?

Accidents do happen.

But so does murder.

Funar was grooming trails and driving snow cats his entire life. He grew up on that mountain, skied it and groomed it for four decades. He knew every trail, bump and tree on the slopes.

What would I do in Funar's place, Rollie thought? I'm grooming trails late at night. The light snow suddenly turns into a blinding squall. I've been doing this my entire life, so what do I do?

The snow cat is heated and comfortable.

Do I continue driving blind?

Or do I shut down and wait for the squall to pass?

I would shut down and wait for the squall to pass.

Funar, on the other hand, might be overconfident in his knowledge of the mountain and his skill driving the snow cat and continue.

I hit a tree. Do I get out in a blinding squall to inspect the damage or do I wait for the squall to pass.

Rollie looked up at his desk and put his hands behind his neck to stretch.

"I wait for the squall to pass," he said aloud. "Because I know better."

•　　•　　•

Before dinner, Rollie presented the girls with a sweatshirt from Vermont and a jug of maple syrup for Mrs. Kravitz.

"Dad, we want to buy the turkey this year," Grace said. "A big, fat Butterball."

Rollie looked at Mrs. Kravitz.

"They grow up so fast," Mrs. Kravitz said.

CHAPTER THIRTY-EIGHT

"Mr. Funar is dead. How is this possible?" Rose said.

Rollie was in Rose's office, seated in a chair opposite the desk. "He had an accident with his snow cat while grooming the ski trails," he said. "At least that's what the official police report says."

"What do you say?" Rose said.

"I think it was murder made to look like an accident," Rollie said.

Rollie could see the fear in Rose's eyes. "This is more than I bargained for," he said.

"It's puzzling alright," Rollie said. "I have to be somewhere, but I'll call you later. And I wouldn't mention this to Enache. No sense worrying the old man."

"I'm going to my cabin in New Hampshire for the holiday," Rose said.

"I know. Have a good time and don't worry," Rollie said. "I'm on top of things. I'll call you with any new information. Oh, and make sure you bring your gun."

•   •   •

The building Marks owned and lived in was an absolute palace. Brass and Gold and etched frosted glass doors were manned by a doorman dressed in a custom-made uniform.

Rollie parked his car in a lot on Fifth Avenue and walked to the Marks Tower a few blocks north.

As he approached the front door, the doorman opened the door and stepped outside and looked at Rollie. "Lieutenant Finch," he said.

"Bob?" Rollie said. "Bob O'Brien?"

"It's me, Lieutenant," O'Brien said.

"You retired from Vice, what, five years ago?" Rollie said.

"More like six," O'Brien said. "I heard you pulled the pin also."

"After my wife died."

"I was sorry to hear that."

"Thanks."

"So, what are you doing here?" O'Brien said.

Rollie showed O'Brien his credentials. "Private, huh," O'Brien said.

"I've been hired by the law firm Marks retained," Rollie said. "Maybe you could help with some questions?"

"I don't see why not."

"What can you tell me about Marks?"

"You mean personally?"

"Anything at all."

"For a billionaire he was a pretty regular guy," O'Brien said. "If I was on the early shift, he'd come down with a coffee mug like any other slob on his way to work and say hello while he waited for his limo. If I'm working nights, he got out of his limo and always said goodnight."

"What about his wife?"

"Justine," O'Brien said. "Between two old cops, right?"

"Between two old cops," Rollie said.

"I thought my first wife was a bitch, but Justine takes the cake," O'Brien said. "She acts like it cost her money to say hello."

"Ever see them argue in public?" Rollie said.

"I've seen her scream and yell at him in public," O'Brien said. "On more than one occasion she'd rip into him and he'd take it like a beaten dog."

"She go out a lot when he was working?" Rollie said.

"Sure. Mostly shopping," O'Brien said. "Two, three times a week she'd come back with armloads of shopping bags."

"Did she have guests visit when Marks was working?" Rollie said.

"The only one I ever saw visit her was her personal trainer, but I'm here only eight hours a day," O'Brien said. "The investigating detectives and the DA went through the guest sign-in log in the lobby and questioned her because she had a noon session with Mrs. Marks."

"Her?" Rollie said.

"The personal trainer is a woman."

"She'd show up wearing leotards and carrying this large gear bag," O'Brien said.

"Have her name."

"Hold on," O'Brien said.

O'Brien entered the lobby and went to the security desk near the elevators. He returned a few minutes later with a business card.

"She works at that really expensive gym on 61st and Second Avenue," O'Brien said as he handed Rollie the card.

"Thanks, Bob," Rollie said.

"Anytime. Good luck, Lieutenant," O'Brien said.

Walking back to his car, Rollie called Teal on his cell phone. "Feel like a free lunch?" he said.

•　　•　　•

"I broke the news to Rose about Funar," Rollie said as he took a bite of his chicken sandwich.

"And how did he take it?" Teal said and bit into his double-bacon cheeseburger.

"Like a frightened little rabbit," Rollie said.

"For real or an act?"

"If it's an act, he deserves an Academy Award," Rollie said.

"So maybe he's not behind it?" Teal said.

"Maybe."

Teal took another bite of his burger and wiped his chin with a napkin. "But?"

"I don't know," Rollie said. "I'm going to see Waite after lunch, but I won't mention it to Enache. I don't want him having a heart attack on me."

"If not Rose, who?" Teal said. "It's not Funar."

"What if Funar's accident was just that, an accident?" Rollie said.

"You said yourself you didn't believe that," Teal said.

"Want dessert?" Rollie said.

"Who doesn't?" Teal said.

"Do me a favor?" Rollie said.

"There's no such thing as a free lunch," Teal said.

•　　•　　•

"Abbey went shopping with one of my men and the old man is taking a nap," Redford said.

"I came to see you anyway," Rollie said. "Remember the seventh man in Vermont?"

"Yeah."

"I went to Vermont to see him," Rollie said. "He's dead. He had an accident with his snow cat on the mountain."

"Jesus, Rollie," Redford said.

"The thing is I'm not so sure it was an accident," Rollie said.

"You think somebody murdered him? Who?" Redford said.

"I don't know," Rollie said. "But don't mention this to Enache and the granddaughter. We don't want panic."

"I won't."

"Don't even tell them I was here," Rollie said.

"Want me to bring an extra man in the house?" Redford said.

"Not in the house, the street," Rollie said.

"You got it, Rollie," Redford said.

"Call me later," Rollie said.

• • •

The girls were doing their homework at the kitchen table when Rollie arrived home. He grabbed a can of ginger ale and opened it at the sink.

"Dad. As soon as we're done here, we're going to the market and buy the turkey," Grace said. "Even Gloria chipped in from her allowance."

"Want me to go with you?" Rollie said.

"Nope, this is our treat," Grace said.

"You can walk Buddy after we leave," Gloria said.

"Yes ma'am," Rollie said.

He took the ginger ale to the office and started making notes on the day's activities.

What if Rose really didn't know about Funar and had nothing to do with Funar's accident?

So who else knew and who was behind it?

What if Funar's accident really was just that?

"Dad, we're going now," Grace said from the hallway.

"Don't forget Buddy," Gloria said.

Rollie stood up from the desk. "Pick up a six-pack of ginger ale.

I just took the last one."

"Will do, Dad," Grace said.

Rollie grabbed his jacket and the leash and went to Gloria's room. The cat bed was on Gloria's bed, filled with sleeping kittens. Buddy and Mama Cat were curled up together next to Gloria's pillow.

"I hate to break up this cat and dog Woodstock moment, but your master wants me to take you for a walk," Rollie said.

Rollie was halfway through Buddy's walk when his cell phone rang. He removed it from his pocket and checked the number. It was Teal calling.

"You got something so soon?" Rollie said.

"I have to admit that your instincts are as sharp as ever," Teal said.

"So, your free lunch was worth it?"

"I just emailed you the report," Teal said.

"Hold on, the dog needs to poop," Rollie said.

"That's why I want a cat," Teal said and hung up.

•   •   •

Back at his desk, Rollie checked his emails and opened the one from Teal.

Justine's personal trainer had a most unusual name. Savannah Strange. She was thirty-two years old and originally from Georgia.

"That explains the name," Rollie said aloud.

Savannah came to New York fourteen years ago to attend NYU Medical for nursing. She switched to physical education and then got her certification as a personal trainer.

She worked at several Manhattan gyms before clicking with the Tower Spa and Gym on Second Avenue. A membership at the Spa started at $20,000 a year.

"Cost more than my car," Rollie said.

Savannah was fired from her first position as trainer at a low-level gym on 14th Street and Broadway for soliciting sex from a female member.

"As they say in the movies, Bingo," Rollie said.

"Dad, we're back," Grace shouted from the kitchen. "Come see."

Rollie went to the kitchen where an enormous turkey rested on the counter.

"What do you think?" Grace said.

"I think you're going back to the store before it closes," Rollie said.

"Why?" Grace said.

"Because we don't have a roasting pan big enough for a bird this size," Rollie said.

Grace looked at Giselle and Gloria. "Come on, girls," she said.

"I'll put everything away and order some pizzas for tonight," Rollie said.

CHAPTER THIRTY-NINE

Before leaving for the airport, Rollie called Gitter and Schram at their office.

"I have something I want to run down concerning the witness list, but it will have to wait until after Thanksgiving," Rollie said. "But I think it's solid."

"Whatever it is, get it to us as soon as you can," Gitter said.

"Tuesday next week I'll stop by," Rollie said. "By the way did Rose ask you about taking over for him in case something happens to him?"

"He did," Gitter said. "Is he being paranoid or is there something to it?"

"A bit of both."

After speaking with Gitter, Rollie called Teal.

"Unless something dramatic breaks, I'll be taking the holidays off and doing nothing but holiday stuff," Rollie said.

"I'm doing the same until Monday," Teal said.

"Listen, I know this is short notice, but my girls came home with a turkey big enough to feed the Salvation Army," Rollie said. "It's just you and Elizabeth now, why not come to dinner?"

"She made reservations at some tofu joint," Teal said.

"That's un-American," Rollie said. "Ask her and call me back. I'm headed to the airport in a bit to pick up Joanna."

"I'll ask," Teal said. "She'll decide."

Before leaving the office, Rollie checked Joanna's flight and it was scheduled for On Time.

He took Buddy for a walk and then left for the airport. The distance to Kennedy was just a couple of miles, but holiday traffic was always brutal, especially at the on and off ramps into the airport.

Even with traffic, Rollie arrived forty-five minutes early. He grabbed a coffee and a seat and called Redford.

"Hi, Bo, how's it going?" Rollie said.

"Quiet," Redford said.

"What are you doing tomorrow?"

"We're having turkey like everybody else," Redford said. "Just the three of us."

"I'll be with my family for a few days, but if something breaks, call me immediately," Rollie said.

"The most eventful thing around here is when the old man wants to play chess, but I'll call you," Redford said.

After Redford, Rollie called Rose. "Gitter and Schram are prepared to take over the tontine in case something happens to you," Rollie said.

"That's little comfort, I'm afraid," Rose said.

"When are you leaving for New Hampshire?" Rollie said.

"Two o'clock train this afternoon," Rose said.

"How about I pick you up on Tuesday and bring you home?" Rollie said. "We can arrange for Redford to assign you a bodyguard until this is over."

"I accept and I should have thought of that myself," Rose said.

"Relax and I'll see you early on Tuesday," Rollie said.

After hanging up with Rose, Rollie walked to Joanna's gate. He checked the schedule and it was still on time.

Rollie's cell phone rang and when he checked the number, he

was surprised to see it was Elizabeth, Teal's wife.

"Hi, Liz," Rollie said.

"Don't you hi Liz me, you food fiend," Elizabeth said.

"I can..." Rollie said.

"Bill has been on a diet for six months and hasn't lost an ounce," Elizabeth said. "And I know it's all those secret lunches you've been buying him."

"Liz, how long have I known you?" Twenty plus years," Rollie said.

"More. You were Bill's best man."

"I'm not going to deny him a hamburger once in a while," Rollie said.

"The department doctor said he needs to lose ten pounds and lower his cholesterol," Elizabeth said.

"They all say that," Rollie said. "Look, he can't live on lettuce, carrots and cucumbers and neither could I. Why not make regular meals, just smaller portions? You'd save Bill a lot of stress and me a lot of money."

Elizabeth sighed. "What time tomorrow?" she said.

"One," Rollie said. "And let him eat. He can diet tomorrow."

"See you at one," Elizabeth said.

Rollie put his phone away and waited for Joanna's plane to land. Finally, the reader board said it landed and fifteen minutes later, Joanna walked through the gate along with hundreds of other passengers.

When Joanna spotted Rollie, she rushed to him, kissed him and hugged him for thirty seconds.

"The girls at school?" she said.

"All three will be home at three thirty," Rollie said.

"Let's get my luggage and get out of here," Joanna said.

.   .   .

Joanna hopped off Rollie and ran into the shower. "Hurry," she said. "The girls will be home in less than an hour."

Rollie took a quick rinse, then left Joanna in the shower and dressed quickly. He went to the kitchen, made a pot of coffee, and took it to the office. He sat at his desk and called Redford.

"Bo, next week can you assign one of your men to Rose?" Rollie said.

"I thought he was on your suspect list," Redford said.

"You know a better way to keep an eye on somebody?" Rollie said.

"Why next week?"

"He's away for Thanksgiving," Rollie said. "I'll pick him up on Tuesday."

"Round the clock coverage?"

"Until the tontine ends."

"It's going to cost."

"He's willing to pay."

"I'll set it up."

"Thanks, Bo," Rollie said. "And Happy Thanksgiving."

Rollie hung up and went to the living room when the girls burst in and Grace yelled, Joanna, we're here."

"She's in my bedroom," Rollie said. "She wanted to shower and change."

"I'm here," Joanna said as she entered the living room.

The girls surrounded Joanna and tugged her to the hall. "Come see," Gloria said.

Rollie stopped by the kitchen for a can of ginger ale and then went to Gloria's room. Joanna was seated on the bed, holding a kitten. She smiled at Rollie. "They're adorable," she said.

Mama Cat looked at Joanna from the floor with mild amusement, but Buddy, next to Mama Cat, started to whine.

"Don't worry, Buddy, I won't hurt your baby," Joanna said and placed the kitten into the cat bed.

"Girls, let her get unpacked and we'll decide where we're going for dinner," Rollie said.

"We're eating out?" Joanna said.

"Since tomorrow will be spent cooking, why not?" Rollie said.

"So, we should change?" Grace said.

"I recommend it," Rollie said.

While the girls changed, Rollie and Joanna went to the kitchen. Rollie filled two cups with coffee and they sat at the table.

"And what surprises have you in store for me?" Joanna said.

"They're not surprises if I tell you," Rollie said. "But, while the girls change, Buddy needs a walk around the block."

"I'll get my coat," Joanna said.

"And I'll get Buddy," Rollie said.

Rollie and Joanna held hands as they took Buddy for a walk around the block.

"Watching the dog poop may not be the best time to bring this up, Rollie, but we need to talk about our relationship," Joanna said.

"I know," Rollie said.

"I've waited a long time since my husband died for a man I can honestly relate to, and I want to make sure you feel the same," Joanna said.

"You're the first woman I've been with since my wife died five years ago," Rollie said.

"So, where are we going?" Joanna said.

"At the moment wherever Buddy takes us," Rollie said.

"Oh no you don't," Joanna said. "You're not joking your way out of this."

"I know," Rollie said. "I also know that long distance relationships never work out, so one of us has to make a dramatic change."

"You have a big house and three girls to put through school," Joanna said. "I'm alone."

"But you're a teacher and you have a responsibility to your school and students," Rollie said. "I'm retired and my pension goes where I go and I can always get a private investigator's license in South Carolina."

"At their age it wouldn't be fair or right to uproot them and ask them to start over in new schools and make new friends," Joanna said. "If one of us has to relocate to make this work it should be me. That is if you want it to work."

"I do and we should talk about it over the next four days," Rollie said.

"Agreed," Joanna said.

"Right now, let's take the girls to dinner," Rollie said.

"Also agreed," Rollie said.

CHAPTER FORTY

"Rollie, are you asleep?" Joanna whispered when she tiptoed into the garage to the daybed.

"No. What time is it?" Rollie said.

"Just after midnight. Move over."

Rollie scooted over a bit and Joanna got into bed next to him.

"Why aren't you asleep?" she said.

"It's not the most comfortable bed," Rollie said.

"At the risk of falling out of this tiny bed, are you in the mood for a nightcap?" Joanna said.

"I thought you'd never ask," Rollie said.

•   •   •

With the girls, Joanna and Mrs. Kravitz in the kitchen, Rollie retreated to the quiet of his office.

Sipping coffee, he opened the file on Savannah Strange. As a personal trainer at the Tower Spa, she couldn't be making much more than twenty dollars an hour. Where she made her money was on home visits for personal workouts. The Tower Spa website listed her services. Fifty dollars bought you thirty minutes of at home personal training. Seventy-five dollars got you an hour. One hundred and thirty-five dollars got you three half-hour visits a week and two hundred dollars got you three sixty-minute sessions.

Savannah averaged fifteen thirty-minute sessions a week, and ten sixty-minute sessions. On average, she raked in fifteen hundred a week not counting tips, more than double her income from the gym.

She lived in a two-bedroom apartment on 86th and Third Avenue with one roommate.

Rollie closed the file when he heard Teal and Elizabeth arrive. He left the office to greet them.

By the time Rollie reached the living room, Gloria was bringing Elizabeth to her bedroom to see the kittens Teal wanted to adopt.

Joanna looked at Rollie and Teal. "Go do your men talk while we set the table," she said.

Rollie and Teal went to Rollie's office and he closed the door.

"The file you sent on the Savannah woman, she's big on my radar," Rollie said.

"You wouldn't have asked for it otherwise," Teal said.

"Feel like doing some poking around with me next week?" Rollie said.

"On the QT only," Teal said.

"Let's make it Wednesday," Rollie said. "I have to pick Rose up on Tuesday and get him a bodyguard from Redford."

"A bodyguard?" Teal said. "Is there something to his frightened rabbit routine?"

"Let's just say it's a chance I'd rather not take," Rollie said. "And besides, what better way to keep an eye on him."

"The keep your friends close bullshit from The Godfather," Teal said.

"Something like that," Rollie said.

"Elizabeth chew you out?" Teal said.

"Something like that."

"We better join the women," Teal said.

The formal table in the dining room was rarely used since Rollie's wife passed away. It expanded to hold a dozen people, so eight fit comfortably. Rollie used an electric knife to carve the turkey and dinner started at 1:30.

Elizabeth kept an eye on Teal, who ate modest portions of everything. Conversation varied from the kittens, to Joanna, to school to the three pies baked by Mrs. Kravitz.

At three o'clock, Rollie and Joanna took Buddy for a walk while the girls cleared the table and Teal and Elizabeth played with the kittens.

Rollie and Joanna held hands as thy walked Buddy around the block.

"I have an idea," Rollie said.

"Does it involve food?"

"In a way," Rollie said. "It also involves travel."

"Christmas. Yes, I was thinking the same thing," Joanna said.

"I was thinking we could go to you this time," Rollie said.

"At my house?" Joanna said. "With my mother there, I hardly have room."

"We'll stay at a nearby motel," Rollie said. "We'll do Christmas Eve and Christmas day at your house and sleep at the motel."

"And the dog and cat?"

"Mrs. Kravitz will house sit," Rollie said. "I already cleared it with her."

"Well," Joanna said. "What would you like for Christmas dinner?"

"Let's get through dessert first," Rollie said.

Mrs. Kravitz baked an apple pie, pumpkin pie, and blueberry pie. The girls baked tollhouse cookies, dark chocolate brownies and made fresh whipped cream.

Teal ate slivers of each pie with one spoon of whipped cream, one cookie and one brownie under the watchful eye of Elizabeth.

Afterward, the girls did the dishes while Joanna, Elizabeth and Mrs. Kravitz took coffee to the living room.

Rollie and Teal took coffee to Rollie's office.

"So, what do you want to do Wednesday?" Teal said.

"Pay a visit to Savannah," Rollie said. "According to the logbook at the Marks building, she had a noon session with Justine Marks."

"And she was cleared by the investigating detectives and the DA," Teal said.

"For lack of evidence," Rollie said. "Not lack of suspicion. The hunting knife, they checked to see if Marks purchased it, but did they check if Savannah purchased it?"

"I don't know," Teal said.

"Find out," Rollie said.

Teal nodded.

"I'll check tomorrow," Teal said.

"We better get back," Rollie said.

Teal and Elizabeth said goodnight at six o'clock and Mrs. Kravitz left shortly thereafter.

Rollie, Joanna, and the girls watched *It's a Wonderful Life* on television. By ten o'clock, the girls were exhausted and went to bed.

"It's been a long day," Joanna said.

"Certainly has," Rollie said.

"I'll see you around midnight," Joanna whispered.

CHAPTER FORTY-ONE

Friday was reserved for a late brunch and then a trip to Rockefeller Center to watch the tree lights come on a five o'clock. After that Rollie led the girls and Joanna to the window displays at Bergdorf Goodman on 5ᵗʰ Avenue, Macy's and Bloomingdale's and finally to Saks Fifth Avenue.

Saturday, they took in the Christmas Show at Radio City Music Hall, followed by dinner at the New York Grill and Deli on First Avenue.

On Sunday Rollie made breakfast at eleven and they took Joanna to the airport at two for her four o'clock flight home.

The girls seemed visibly upset and sad to see Joanna leave.

"Girls, you father and I have been talking and, well, how would you like to spend Christmas with me in South Carolina?" Joanna said.

Of course, it was unanimous.

On the way home, Grace said, "We need to go shopping for South Carolina clothes."

•   •   •

Rollie brought a mug of coffee to his office and then called Rose on his cell phone.

"How are you doing?" Rollie said.

"Jumping at every little noise," Rose said.

"Who else knows where you are?" Rollie said.

"Besides you, no one."

"Try to relax," Rollie said. "I'll pick you up Tuesday around noon. I made arrangements with Redford for a bodyguard."

"I guess I got more than I bargained for," Rose said.

"Like I said, try to relax," Rollie said.

After hanging up with Rose, Rollie changed into sweats and did thirty minutes of the step climber and another thirty on the Bowflex.

After the workout, he found the girls sulking in the living room.

"What?" he said.

"Nothing," Grace said.

"We miss Joanna," Gloria said.

"She isn't even home yet," Rollie said.

"We miss her anyway," Gloria said.

"We'll see her in a month," Rollie said. "In the meantime, you guys haven't eaten since breakfast."

"We're not hungry," Giselle said.

"I guess I'll order a small pizza for myself then," Rollie said.

"Hey, wait," Gloria said.

.   .   .

Rollie emerged from the shower to find the girls talking to Joanna. He told Grace to tell her he'd call back on his cell phone.

Rollie dressed and took a can of ginger ale to his office and called Joanna.

"I had a wonderful time," Joanna said. "I miss you and the girls."

"The girls are miserable," Rollie said. "They're moping."

"And you? Are you moping?" Joanna said.

"I have to admit, a bit," Rollie said.

"We're fix that come Christmas," Joanna said.

They chatted for a while and by the time Rollie hung up, three large pizzas with a dozen garlic rolls arrived.

"We talked about details," Rollie said as he opened the boxes at the kitchen table. "Joanna will have her mother for Christmas and her house is small, so we're staying at a motel. Is that okay with you guys?"

"Will it have a pool?" Grace said. "I want to be able to say I went swimming on Christmas morning."

"We'll need new bathing suits," Giselle said.

"And South Carolina clothes," Grace said.

"Pass me a garlic roll," Rollie said.

CHAPTER FORTY-TWO

"**Your instincts are as** sharp as ever," Teal said as Rollie set two containers of coffee on Teal's desk.

"What do you have?" Rollie said.

"I checked Savannah Strange's credit cards going back three years and there are no purchases for hunting knives," Teal said. "However, her roommate Claire Fulkers is a professional rock-climbing instructor and she purchased a Buck 120 General Knife with a seven and three-quarter inch blade at a store in upstate New York about four years ago. It's the exact same knife as the one that killed Justine Marks."

"Odds that if we talked to Fulkers her knife is missing?" Rollie said.

"I wouldn't take that bet," Teal said.

"Can you get a search warrant?" Rollie said.

"I'm going to see a judge right now," Teal said.

"I'll meet you at Fulkers's apartment in two hours," Rollie said. "No sense waiting until Wednesday."

•   •   •

"Fuck a duck," Schram said when Rollie broke the news.

"Where's your car, Rollie?" Gitter said.

"Downstairs at a meter," Rollie said.

"Let's go," Gitter said.

.　　.　　.

"I don't understand. I told you I lost that knife months ago," Claire Fulkers said.

Teal, Rollie, Gitter, Schram and Fulkers sat at the kitchen table while four uniformed officers conducted a search of the apartment.

"Where?" Teal said.

"I don't know," Fulkers said. "On a climb somewhere. How do I know? I lost it is all I know."

"What did you need a knife like that for anyway?" Teal said.

"Mister, have you ever been on a climb?" Fulkers said.

"I have," Rollie said.

"You have?" Teal said.

"In the Army," Rollie said. "And if you get in trouble on a climb and you need to cut your pack loose or free a rope, you better have a good knife handy."

"Exactly right," Fulkers said.

"Did you replace the knife?" Rollie said.

"I did. I purchased a Gerber Survival Knife," Fulkers said. "It's with my gear in my bedroom."

A uniformed officer entered the kitchen with a long sheath. "We found this is Miss Savage's gym gear," he said.

"That's for my missing Buck," Fulkers said. "That bitch."

"Captain Teal, perhaps you should bring Miss Savage in for questioning?" Gitter said.

.　　.　　.

209

"The personal trainer?" Marks said as he slumped into a chair opposite Rollie.

They were at the conference table in Gitter and Schram's office.

"The police picked her up three hours ago," Gitter said. "She made a full confession."

"She was having an affair with your wife, I'm afraid," Schram said. "Your wife wanted to break it off. Miss Savage didn't."

"Jesus," Marks said.

"We'll be going to court in the morning, along with the DA to drop all charges against you," Gitter said.

"And for what this is worth, none of this would be happening without him," Schram said and nodded to Rollie.

"We suggest you pay the man what he's worth," Gitter said.

•   •   •

Rollie watched the news while Gloria did her homework in the kitchen. The story of the day was the startling arrest of Savannah Strange for the murder of billionaire real estate developer Robert Marks's wife Justine.

Assistant Chief of Detectives William Teal held a press conference in front of One Police Plaza and answered questions.

Rollie turned off the television and went to the kitchen.

"Almost done?" he said.

"Just about," Gloria said.

"Let's take Buddy for a walk," Rollie said. "And then we'll start dinner."

•   •   •

After Buddy's walk, Rollie went to his office for a bit and called

Redford.

"Bo, I'm picking up Rose tomorrow," Rollie said. "Do you have a man assigned to protect him?"

"Mike Thomas, remember him?" Redford said.

"I do."

"He's a good man," Redford said.

"Okay. Have him meet us at Rose's townhouse late tomorrow afternoon."

"Will do, Rollie."

Rollie hung up and went to the kitchen where Gloria was setting the table.

"The house feels kind of empty without Joanna," Gloria said.

"In three weeks and two days, you can tell her that," Rollie said. "Your sisters will be home in one hour, let's start dinner."

A few minutes later, as Rollie was cutting carrots and Gloria was peeling potatoes, Teal called on the hard line.

"Did you watch the press conference?" Teal said.

"I did," Rollie said.

"I did as you asked and kept you out of it," Teal said.

"Thank you for that," Rollie said.

"I got a big pat on the back and a key to the all boys club," Teal said. "And I feel pretty rotten taking credit for your work."

"You got a key and I got a check for $50,000," Rollie said.

"In that case, the next lunch is on you," Teal said.

"When have you ever paid for lunch?" Rollie said.

"Bye, Rollie," Teal said and hung up.

CHAPTER FORTY-THREE

Rollie left home at 8:00 in the morning, shortly after Grace drove her sisters to school. He set the GPS for Rose's address on Lake Winnipesauke in New Hampshire and took the New England Thruway North.

He stopped once at a rest stop for coffee and then drove straight through into New Hampshire. The lake was the largest in New Hampshire and nestled in the foothills of the White Mountains.

To reach Rose's lakeside cottage, Rollie had to drive through the town of Laconia, a small, but popular ski and resort town.

A mile around the lake and Rollie pulled into the driveway of Rose's lakefront cottage. It was a quaint, stone cottage with a red brick chimney. Rollie left the car and knocked on the door.

When Rose didn't answer, Rollie called his cell phone. After six rings, the call went to voicemail.

Rollie returned to his car to wait. It was possible that Rose took a cab to town.

But Rose knew he would be here by noon.

Rollie tried Rose's cell phone twice more, spacing the calls fifteen minutes apart.

At one o'clock in the afternoon, Rollie called 911.

At 1:20, two state troopers picked the lock to Rose's front door and entered the house where they found Rose in his bathtub. His eyes were closed and he was obviously dead. His newly purchased gun was on the nightstand beside the bed.

"I talked to him Sunday night," Rollie said. "We made arrangements for me to pick him up at noon today."

"It could be a heart attack," a trooper said.

"Or possible drug overdose," the other trooper said.

While EMTs took the body to the morgue, Rollie went to the state barracks and spoke with a detective.

Rollie and the detective spoke for more than two hours.

"It's quite possible Mr. Rose was murdered for the reasons you say," the detective said. "It is also possible he died of natural causes. There are no signs of forced entry or a struggle and nothing is out of place or apparently missing."

"The medical examiner will find water in his lungs indicating he drowned," Rollie said. "He was a little man. It wouldn't have been difficult to hold his head under water."

"I'll let you know," the detective said.

"Send a copy of the report to Assistant Chief of Detectives Bill Teal," Rollie said. "He was assisting me on this."

"I will," the detective said.

•　　•　　•

Rollie stopped somewhere on the Mass Turnpike for coffee. He called home and spoke to Grace.

"I'll be late," he said. "Just wanted to let you know."

"We'll hold dinner," Grace said.

"Thank you, sweetheart," Rollie said.

"Dad, is everything okay? You sound tired," Grace said.

"I'm just a little tired from driving is all," Rollie said. "I'll be home around eight."

After hanging up with Grace, Rollie called Gitter and Schram.

"Put this on speaker," Rollie said.

"We're both here," Gitter said.

"Rose is dead," Rollie said. "You get to handle the tontine money."

"What?" Schram said.

"How?" Gitter said.

"He drowned in his bathtub in New Hampshire," Rollie said.

"Accidental?" Gitter said.

"Someone made it look that way," Rollie said.

"Jesus Christ," Schram said.

"I'll stop by your office sometime tomorrow and you can sign whatever you need giving you authority over the funds," Rollie said.

"Which paints a target on our backs," Gitter said.

"Whoever killed Rose would have to know who you are and that information hasn't been made public," Rollie said.

"Maybe you can make some sense of this because we can't," Schram said.

"I'll see you in the morning," Rollie said.

Next, he called Redford.

"Cancel your guy Thomas," Rollie said.

"How come?" Redford said.

"Because Rose is dead," Rollie said.

"Dead? I thought you were bringing him home today."

"I was. He drowned in the bathtub."

"Get out of here. Nobody drowns in a bathtub," Redford said.

"They do if they're murdered," Rollie said.

"Shit. So, what now?"

"We keep Enache alive for two more weeks," Rollie said. "If there is room, bring Thomas in so there are two of you round the clock."

"I can do that," Redford said.

"Don't say anything just yet," Rollie said. "I'll be there tomorrow and I'll break the news myself."

"The old man has a doctor's appointment at ten for a checkup," Redford said.

"I'll stop by around eleven thirty," Rollie said.

"See you then."

Rollie hung up, started the car, and drove to Manhattan.

•　　•　　•

"Are you fucking kidding me?" Teal said.

"I wish I was," Rollie said.

Teal sat back in his chair and reached for the container of coffee Rollie brought him. "So, the little lawyer wasn't guilty after all," he said.

"Eight dead over this money," Rollie said. "And someone is out there waiting to make it nine."

"If you mean the eighty-six-year-old, it's highly unlikely he killed anybody," Teal said.

"You're going to receive the ME report from New Hampshire," Rollie said.

"Nothing like a little light reading," Teal said.

"I have to get home," Rollie said.

•　　•　　•

The girls waited for Rollie to arrive home so they could eat dinner together.

"Hard day?" Grace said.

"Nothing a good dinner and eight hours sleep won't cure," Rollie said.

After dinner, while the girls did the dishes and tidied the kitchen,

Rollie took a cup of coffee to his office.

Who the hell murdered John Henry Rose Junior?

His silent partner? The man he hired to do the dirty work? Could it be possible that this man, whoever he was, made a better deal with Enache?

Or was Enache behind it all along as Rollie first assumed?

But why kill Rose as this late stage with just a few weeks to go to claim the prize?

Say Rose was to collect ten percent for his end. Enache would save over a million dollars by having Rose killed.

But who did the killing?

It certainly wasn't Enache, so who?

And how did they locate Rose at his New Hampshire cottage?

Was he followed?

Was he…?

Rollie snatched up his cell phone and called Redford.

"Rollie, is—" Redford said.

"Sweep the house for bugs," Rollie said. "Tonight. Right now."

"Jesus," Redford said.

"Call me back."

Rollie hung up and called Teal at home.

"Don't you ever stop thinking?" Teal said.

"No. Get a warrant from a judge tomorrow to enter Rose's townhouse so we can search for wiretaps," Rollie said.

There was a long pause. Rollie could sense Teal thinking.

Then Teal said, "Fuck."

"Call me when you got it," Rollie said.

Rollie went to the kitchen for fresh coffee and then found the girls watching a movie in the living room. A remake of *The Call of the Wild*.

"Please tell me the dog doesn't die," Gloria said.

"No, but everybody else does," Rollie said.

"As long as the dog lives," Gloria said.

"You got school tomorrow," Rollie said.

"We know," Grace said. "Bed as soon as the movie is over."

Rollie returned to his office, sat at his desk, and waited. Around 10:15, the girls came in to say goodnight.

Forty-five minutes later, Redford called Rollie's cell phone.

"Bingo," Redford said.

"How many?"

"Three."

"See you tomorrow," Rollie said.

CHAPTER FORTY-FOUR

Rollie and Teal watched as a locksmith unlocked the front door to Rose's townhouse. Four detectives waited behind them.

"All yours," the locksmith said.

Teal opened the door. "You men take the apartment upstairs," he said as he and Rollie put on latex gloves.

The four detectives took the stairs while Rollie and Teal entered the office on the first floor.

Originally a six-room apartment, just the kitchen remained functional. The other four rooms served as storage space. Rollie and Teal started in the kitchen. While Teal searched cabinets, Rollie made a pot of coffee.

"He's got better appliances in his office kitchen than I do at home," Teal said. "Look at this toaster. Must cost a hundred bucks."

Under the cabinets was a track light and Rollie felt under the cabinets and across the track. Somewhere in the middle of the track, Rollie removed a small, magnetic transmitter.

Teal inspected it. "You can buy these at Radio Shack," he said.

Rollie poured two cups of coffee while Teal removed the tiny battery from the transmitter.

"Something an amateur would do," Rollie said.

"An amateur didn't kill eight people without being detected," Teal said.

"Let's check the office," Teal said.

A thorough search of the office produced one additional transmitter hidden behind a file cabinet. It was identical to the one from the kitchen.

One of the detectives entered the office. "Captain, we found three transmitters upstairs," he said. "One in the living room, kitchen and bedroom."

"Everywhere he might talk on the phone," Teal said.

"What about the bathroom?" Rollie said.

"That's next."

After the detective went back upstairs, Rollie and Teal checked the bathroom on the first floor. Designed for an apartment, the bathroom was large with a shower, tub, linen closet, and medicine cabinet above the sink.

Rollie found a transmitter above the medicine cabinet.

"Makes three," Teal said.

Rollie put the transmitter into a plastic baggie along with the others.

They returned to the kitchen for another cup of coffee and sat at the table.

"Alright if not Rose, who?" Teal said.

"Whoever planted these transmitters," Rollie said.

The four detectives entered the kitchen. "We found one more in the bathroom," a detective said.

"Seven altogether," Teal said. "Take the three we found to the lab. Check them for prints and see if you can locate where they came from."

"Sure thing, Captain," a detective said.

"I'll be in Brooklyn," Teal said.

•　　•　　•

Rollie and Teal looked at the three transmitters Redford found in the Enache home.

"Where?" Rollie said.

"Kitchen, bathroom and living room," Redford said.

"Identical to the ones we found," Teal said.

"Where's Enache?" Rollie said.

"He was tired after the doctor visit," Redford said. "He's taking a nap."

"And the granddaughter?" Rollie said.

"She went grocery shopping with Thomas," Redford said. "Rollie, what the fuck is going on?"

"Someone is clearing a path for Enache to inherit the twelve million," Rollie said.

"But Rose was the man signing the money over," Redford said. "What sense does it make killing him?"

"Good question. No answer," Rollie said.

"Besides Rollie, have there been any calls?" Teal said.

"Not on the hard-line," Redford said. "I can't answer for the girl. When she isn't doting on the old man, she's in her room."

"Don't tell her or Enache about Rose just yet," Rollie said. "I need to do a few things first."

"Sure," Redford said.

"And if you find any more transmitters call me right away," Rollie said.

"Will do," Redford said.

●　　●　　●

Gitter and Schram signed the documents assuming control of the tontine funds.

"Who and why kill Rose," Schram said. "The man never harmed

so much as a bug in his life."

"And what about us?" Gitter said. "Suppose whoever killed Rose comes after us next?"

"They won't," Rollie said.

"They won't show themselves again until after Enache gets the money," Rollie said. "And without you two to sign the money over that won't happen."

"Small comfort," Gitter said.

"Have you told Mr. Enache about Rose?" Schram said.

"No. I don't want the old man do die from a heart attack before he collects," Rollie said.

"We'll go before him the way this is going," Gitter said.

"It's all over in twelve days," Rollie said.

"What are the police doing to find this mysterious serial killer?" Schram said.

"I'll let you know," Rollie said.

．　　　．　　　．

While the girls prepared dinner in the kitchen, Rollie made notes at his desk in the office.

Teal called on Rollie's cell phone.

"Hell of a day," Teal said.

"Yeah."

"Got the medical examiner's report from New Hampshire," Teal said. "Rose drowned as you said. They found traces of skin and blood under his fingernails."

"He put up a fight," Rollie said.

"Yeah, but against whom?" Teal said.

"Anything else in the report?"

"Traces of latex in his hair and neck."

"The killer wore latex gloves," Rollie said.

"The report on the cottage is bare bones," Teal said. "No fingerprints anywhere except for Rose. Every window and door is intact, so how did the killer get inside?"

"Time of death?" Rollie said.

"ME puts it at around ten the night before," Teal said.

"Any thing from his townhouse?" Rollie said.

"My team dusted every square inch," Teal said. "And found a thousand prints in the office and just his in the apartment upstairs and traces of latex on doors and also the transmitters."

"Hairs, fibers, traces of footsteps?" Rollie said.

"Just his," Teal said.

"The money is released in twelve days," Rollie said. "Gitter and Schram agreed to handle the paperwork in Rose's absence."

"This is going to come down to blind luck," Teal said.

"Or a stupid mistake," Rollie said. "Or both."

"What are you doing tomorrow?" Teal said.

"Thinking," Rollie said.

"Keep doing that, it's what you're good at," Teal said.

Rollie left the office and went to the kitchen.

"Dinner is ready," Grace said.

"Thanks, girls," Rollie said.

"Dad, we're going shopping on Saturday to pick up a few things for South Carolina," Grace said.

"We looked up the weather for December," Giselle said. "It's around seventy degrees during the day and around forty-five at night."

"We'd like to swim in the pool at the motel, but also have something warm for at night," Gloria said.

"What's wrong with the clothes you have?" Rollie said.

"You're a man," Grace said.

"What does that have to do…" Rollie said.

"You have no fashion sense," Gloria said.

"And it wouldn't hurt you none to pick up a few new shirts for the trip," Grace said.

"What's wrong with the shirts I have?" Rollie said.

"Really, Dad?" Grace said.

"We talked it over and we're taking you to the mall with us on Sunday," Gloria said.

"You want me to go to a mall in December?" Rollie said.

"One time isn't going to kill you," Grace said.

Rollie sighed, which was his sign of defeat.

"We made dessert," Grace said.

CHAPTER FORTY-FIVE

Every time Rollie drifted off to sleep, his brain jump-started him awake with questions. Questions he had no answers to.

Around 2:00 in the morning, Rollie got out of bed and went to the kitchen. He filled a glass with milk and took a bag of chocolate chip cookies from a cabinet and sat at the table.

He dunked a cookie in the milk and took a bite.

How was somebody able to gain access to Rose's townhouse, cottage, and Enache's home in Brooklyn sight unseen?

In his robe pocket, Rollie always kept a small notepad and pencil. He took them out and scribbled a note.

Ask New Hampshire State Police to check the cottage for transmitters.

"What are you doing, Dad?" Grace said as she entered the kitchen.

"Having cookies and milk," Rollie said.

Grace filled a glass with milk, sat and grabbed a cookie.

"You have school in the morning," Rollie said.

"I know," Grace said as she dunked a cookie.

"How come you guys are up?" Giselle said as she walked into the kitchen.

"We're having cookies," Grace said.

Giselle filled a glass with milk, sat beside grace and grabbed a cookie.

"There's only one left," Grace said.

Giselle stood and removed a second bag from the cabinet and set it on the table just as Gloria wandered into the kitchen.

"What's going on, we have school tomorrow?" Gloria said.

"Cookies and milk," Giselle said.

Gloria filled a glass with milk and sat beside Giselle.

"You need a new robe, Dad," Gloria said.

"It's on the list for when we go to the mall," Grace said.

"Pass me a cookie," Rollie said.

. . .

After breakfast and the girls had left for school, Rollie took a mug of coffee to his office and called Teal.

"I couldn't sleep last night," Rollie said.

"Same problem," Teal said. "The doctor said it's my prostate. He said I should take a supplement called—"

"Call the New Hampshire State Police and ask them to do a sweep of Rose's cottage for transmitters," Rollie said.

"That kept you up all night?"

"Among other things," Rollie said. "Listen, get phone records for the townhouse, cottage and Enache's home going back three months."

"You think the killer called all three?" Teal said.

"There are only two ways the killer entered the cottage, the townhouse and Enache's home in Brooklyn," Rollie said. "The first is with a key."

"And the second?" Teal said.

"He was invited in," Rollie said.

"I'll call New Hampshire and get the phone records," Teal said.

"Call me when you get them," Rollie said.

After hanging up with Teal, Rollie took Buddy for a walk around the block. Still restless, he changed into sweats and went to the garage for a workout. He upped the step-climber to forty-five minutes and the same for the Bowflex.

Covered in sweat, Rollie took a shower and changed into a comfortable warm-up suit and went to the kitchen. He fixed a peanut butter and jelly and banana sandwich, filled a glass with milk and returned to his office.

He thought and waited for Teal to call back as he ate. Sandwich and milk consumed, Rollie washed the plate and glass in the sink and then went to Gloria's room.

Buddy and Mama Cat were asleep on the bed. The kittens were asleep in the cat bed on the floor. Buddy looked up at Rollie and Rollie scratched his ear.

"Resume guard duty," Rollie said, and left the bedroom.

Teal called at three o'clock while Rollie was at his desk, making notes.

"Got phone records," Teal said. "Three months ago, a dozen calls from Rose to Enache and almost as many from Enache to Rose."

"Consistent with Rose breaking the news to Enache," Rollie said.

"Two months ago, more of the same, but not as much," Teal said. "Last month just one call from Enache to Rose."

"Cell records?" Rollie said.

"Enache doesn't have one," Teal said. "And Rose has dozens of calls a day, presumably from clients."

"Can you fax the list to my computer?" Rollie said.

"Sure."

"Thanks, Bill," Rollie said.

Rollie hung up and called Redford.

"How's it going, Bo?" Rollie said.

"Thomas and the girl went to the drug store to pick up the old man's prescriptions and the old man is napping," Redford said.

"Bo, do you have Abbey's cell number?" Rollie said.

"Hold on, it's in my phone," Redford said. "Here it is."

Redford read the number to Rollie, who wrote it in his notepad.

"Thanks, Bo," Rollie said.

"Is something wrong?" Redford said.

"No, I accidentally deleted some contact numbers," Rollie said. "I'll call you later."

Rollie hung up and went to the living room when the girls arrived home from school.

"Buddy needs a walk," Gloria said.

"I'll go with you," Rollie said.

Rollie grabbed his jacket and he and Gloria took Buddy for a walk around the block.

"I'm kind of worried about Buddy and the cats when we go to North Carolina," Gloria said.

"Mrs. Kravitz will take good care of them," Rollie said.

"I know, but what if something happens?" Gloria said.

"She'll call us if something happens, but if it makes you feel better, we can check with her every day," Rollie said.

Back in the office, Rollie downloaded the phone records Teal sent and while the girls did their homework, Rollie scanned the numbers.

Rose had a ton of calls to his office and cell phone, but that wasn't surprising as he had a thousand or more clients.

He read through the numbers, scanning for something odd, something out of place, but nothing clicked.

He cross-referenced numbers, searching for a link, but again, nothing clicked.

Frustrated, Rollie went to the kitchen where the girls were doing their homework. "Girls, what say we skip cooking and go out tonight?" he said.

"Sure, Dad," Grace said.

"Where do you want to go?" Giselle said.

"I'll let you girls pick," Rollie said. "Be ready by six thirty."

"Sure, Dad," Grace said.

Rollie took a fresh cup of coffee to the office, sat behind his desk, and called Joanna at home.

"I just walked in the door," Joanna said. "Hold on while I kick off my shoes."

Rollie sipped coffee, and a few seconds later, Joanna came back on the line. "I ordered a real tree," she said. "I thought we could decorate it on Christmas Eve. My mother has a ton of decorations."

"Sounds good. The girls haven't decorated a tree since their mother died," Rollie said.

"I haven't had one since my divorce," Joanna said.

"I'd say it's about time we started living again," Rollie said.

"I say, I agree," Joanna said.

"We'll be at the motel around five in the afternoon on the 23rd," Rollie said. "I'd like to take you and your mom to dinner."

"Sounds good," Joanna said. "She'll be here Tuesday. School is out at noon on the 23rd, so we can meet you at the motel if you'd like."

"I'll call you when we get there," Rollie said.

They chatted for a bit more and then Rollie turned his attention back to the phone numbers.

Many were repeat numbers from clients with calls going back and forth.

The last call Rose took before he was killed was from Rollie himself. The, don't worry; I'll pick you up on Tuesday call.

Rollie flipped the pages, reading numbers until his eyes were blurry. He quit at six o'clock and went to his bedroom to change.

The girls wanted Italian and he drove them to the Roma on

Queens Boulevard. Over plates of pasta and meatballs, Rollie told the girls about the Christmas tree.

"Dad, we have to get you some new slacks and shirts to wear for South Carolina," Grace said.

"Joanna must think you shop only at the thrift store," Giselle said.

"There's nothing wrong with the way I..." Rollie said.

The girls laughed and rolled their eyes.

"Pass me a garlic roll," Rollie said.

CHAPTER FORTY-SIX

Rollie was driven whenever he was stumped. He was that way as a homicide detective and he was that way now.

He would spend entire days on a detail that did not make sense or fit the scenario. About ten years ago, he drew a homicide case where the prime suspect was the husband, because a mother just couldn't murder her own baby daughter. The couple was separated. The baby was just thirteen months old. The mother lived in a walk-up apartment in Washington Heights near the GW Bridge. The father lived at the YMCA. One afternoon, as the mother pushed the baby in her stroller through a park in the neighborhood, she called 911 and reported that someone kidnapped her baby.

The mother claimed the father stole her baby. Everybody said the husband was no good, that he needed money and kidnapped the baby and sold her on the black market.

The father had no alibi. He was a suspect after no ransom demands came forward.

What bothered Rollie most were the lack of details. No one in the crowded park could remember seeing the mother and her baby that day. People in her building saw her leave with the stroller, but never actually saw the baby.

The mother played the victim perfectly and the media convicted the husband in their headlines.

But something didn't ring true and Rollie switched focus to the mother. She was twenty-two and attractive and found a new boyfriend, who didn't want children. Afraid of losing her new man, the mother smothered her baby with a pillow and disposed of the body by throwing it into the furnace in the basement of her building.

So, what detail had he missed? What was keeping him awake nights?

Something overlooked. Something so...

Rollie tossed off the covers, slipped on his robe and went to the office. At his desk, he read through the list of phone numbers one more time.

"Wait," he said, aloud.

He scrolled through his cell phone and located the number for Abbey; the one Redford gave him the other day. He didn't really delete it, he never had it. The one missing detail.

She called Rose several times in the beginning and again just a few days before he was murdered.

Why did she call him?

"Jesus Christ," Rollie said.

•　　•　　•

"Last year, Rose got in touch with the seven remaining members of the tontine," Rollie said. "It was a crap shoot at that time as to who would live longest and collect. Abbey saw the opportunity and worked out a deal with Rose to make sure her grandfather would collect the prize. Rose knew the locations of the other six and gave them to Abbey in exchange for a nice cut of the money."

Teal nodded as he bit into his bacon cheeseburger.

"Abbey is a young, strong girl and could easily overpower a man in a nursing home," Rollie said. "One at a time, she clears the field until just Enache remains, except I discover a seventh and now she has to get rid of him, too. Only you, me and Rose had that information."

"So, Rose passes it along to her and bye-bye, Funar," Teal said.

"It adds up," Rollie said.

"What doesn't add up is why hire you and then why kill Rose?" Teal said.

"The rules of the tontine state that every effort possible must be made to establish that the surviving member is the last one and proof must be given to the bank in order to release the funds," Rollie said. "I was window dressing. Rose never believed my theory about a seventh man until I actually found him. After Abbey went to Vermont, she forced Funar to take the snow cat up the mountain and staged the accident. That's when Rose began to panic, thinking she might come after him next, rather than split the money with him."

"She planted the transmitters?" Teal said. "She had access to her home, Rose's home and office."

"Has to be," Rollie said.

"So, she knew Rose was going to New Hampshire ahead of time by listening to his calls," Teal said.

"No other way," Rollie said.

"And he opened the door to her, which explains why no sign of forced entry."

"Has to be."

"Can you prove any of this theory of yours?" Teal said.

"Not one word," Rollie said.

"In a few days, the old man collects twelve million dollars," Teal said. "Any bets he dies of natural causes soon afterward and she inherits the whole shebang?"

"That was her plan all along," Rollie said.

"Want me to bring her in for questioning?" Teal said.

"I have a feeling you'd get nothing out of her," Rollie said.

"She's going to walk," Teal said.

"Pick her up, but let me do the interview," Rollie said.

"I'd have to be in the room with you," Teal said.

"Pick her up outside the house," Rollie said. "We don't want to give the old man a heart attack."

"How do I do that?" Teal said.

"I'll get her outside the house and you pick her up," Rollie said.

"When?"

"No time like the present," Rollie said.

"Let me grab a slice of apple pie first," Teal said.

CHAPTER FORTY-SEVEN

"I need to speak with you privately," Rollie said. "Outside. We might have missed a transmitter somewhere."

"What about?" Abbey said.

"Making arrangements for the money," Rollie said. "It's just a few days away."

"I'll get my coat," Abbey said.

"Want me to go along?" Redford said.

"Stay with the old man," Rollie said.

Abbey got her coat and Rollie walked her outside to the street where Teal and two detectives waited for them.

Teal flashed his badge and identification. "I'm William Teal, Assistant Chief of Detectives and I'd like to ask you some questions," he said.

"What about?" Abbey said.

"It's cold out here," Teal said. "Let's take a ride."

•   •   •

Teal requested the use of an interrogation room at the local precinct in Park Slope. He and Rollie conducted the interview with Abbey.

"You're crazy," Abbey said and laughed.

"I don't think so," Rollie said. "I think you and Rose orchestrated this entire scheme going back a year and then you got rid of Rose because he's weak and you couldn't trust him."

"Like I said, you're crazy," Abbey said. "I'm just a poor girl from Brooklyn, taking care of her grandfather."

"You planted the bugs on Rose and in your own house, so you could listen from another room," Rollie said. "That's how you knew about the seventh man."

"I haven't a clue what you're talking about," Abbey said.

"My function was to prove to the court and the bank that all requirements of the tontine were met, so your grandfather could inherit the twelve million," Rollie said.

"And that has what to do with me?" Abbey said. "I didn't hire you; Rose did."

"The real kick in the teeth came when I actually found a seventh man," Rollie said. "Only Rose and I were aware of that fact, but thanks to your transmitters, so were you."

Abbey grinned at Rollie.

"After that, Rose panicked a bit," Rollie said. "If you could kill Funar so easily, why not kill him to, and keep all the money."

"Is that what you think?" Abbey said. "That I killed Rose?"

"That's what I think," Rollie said.

"Prove it," Abbey said.

"I intend to do just that," Rollie said.

"Let me know when that happens," Abbey said. "In the meantime, I'm going home and see to my grandfather."

Abbey stood up from the interrogation table. "Any objections?" she said.

"You're free to go," Teal said.

"Thanks for a very illuminating afternoon," Abbey said.

• • •

Rollie and Teal stopped at a coffee shop a few blocks from the Brooklyn police station.

"That girl is pure ice water," Teal said.

"She'd have to be to kill eight people in cold blood," Rollie said.

"It fits. All of it," Teal said. "Except there isn't one shred of evidence I can take to a judge for a warrant."

"Maybe you could convince a judge based on circumstantial?" Rollie said.

"And maybe I'll lose weight eating cheeseburgers," Teal said.

"Let's squeeze her," Rollie said. "See if we can rattle her enough to force her hand."

"And how do we do that?" Teal said.

"Start small," Rollie said.

Rollie took out his cell phone and called Redford.

"Bo, the job is over," Rollie said. "Pack up and go home."

"What's going on?" Redford said. "The girl came in crying and went to her room."

"It's not our concern anymore," Rollie said. "You did your job and it's now done so pack up and head home."

"Okay, Rollie," Redford said. "But do I get to know what's going on?"

"In a few days," Rollie said.

Rollie hung up and sipped his coffee.

"She was probably listening in," Rollie said.

Teal nodded. "I could have some of my men stake the place out, see if she gets nervous," he said.

"She murdered eight men, I doubt she's the nervous type," Rollie said. "But give it a try."

"And what are you going to do?" Teal said.

"Think," Rollie said.

CHAPTER FORTY-EIGHT

"You said you wanted to think, but I didn't think you meant from my personal car," Teal said.

Parked across the street from Enache's townhouse, Rollie and Teal kept an eye on the townhouse and the police cruiser parked directly curbside.

"We've been here two hours, she must have spotted the cruiser by now," Teal said.

"She spotted it," Rollie said. "What's she going to do about it is the question."

"How long do you want to sit on this?" Teal said.

"Give it until noon," Rollie said.

Teal glanced at the dashboard clock. "Noon it is," he said.

Forty-five minutes later, Abbey exited the townhouse, walked down the front steps to the sidewalk and walked past the police cruiser without so much as a glance in its direction.

"She's definitely ice water," Teal said.

"Call your guys, tell them to follow," Rollie said.

Teal called the cruiser and told them to follow Abbey.

"And we'll follow them," Rollie said.

Teal started the car and slowly followed the police cruiser that followed Abbey.

Abbey turned the corner and walked away from the park.

"Where's she going?" Teal said.

"My guess is the subway," Rollie said.

"She could be going to the store," Teal said.

"She's going to the subway," Rollie said.

"She knows that cruiser is following her," Teal said. "Not even a glance."

Abbey walked five more blocks and descended the steps to the Fifth Street and Seventh Avenue subway stop.

"You were right," Teal said.

"Call off your boys and I'll buy you lunch," Rollie said.

●　　●　　●

"I haven't been to Junior's Restaurant in twenty years," Teal said.

Famous for its cheesecake, Junior's Restaurant was located close to the Brooklyn Bridge.

Rollie and Teal order the fried chicken basket for lunch.

"Want to take another run at her?" Teal said.

"I don't think it would do a bit of good," Rollie said. "I wanted to test her mettle under pressure and she didn't blink. She didn't blink during interrogation and she didn't blink now."

"If she killed eight men in cold blood, a cruiser isn't going to make a dent in her armor," Teal said.

"No, it isn't," Rollie said. "We'll just have to find another way."

"Such as?"

"What's her motive?" Rollie said.

"The oldest one in the book," Teal said. "Money."

"I don't know if she approached Rose or if Rose approached her, but at this point it doesn't matter," Rollie said. "Enache will inherit the $12,000,000 and shorty thereafter, he will die, leaving her a very rich young woman."

"She'll sell that townhouse for another two million and sail away into the sunset, never to be heard from again," Teal said.

"Money," Rollie said.

"What?" Teal said.

"That's what she wants, that's what we'll give her," Rollie said. "Drop me off at my car."

"We're not giving her a damn thing without a slice of cheesecake first," Teal said.

CHAPTER FORTY-NINE

"**Dad, you promised we** could take you to the mall," Grace said.

At his desk, Rollie said, "Give me ten minutes. We'll take my car."

"I'll warm it up. Ten minutes," Grace said.

"Okay, you drive."

Rollie used his cell phone to call Abbey's cell phone. To his surprise, she answered.

"No police car today," Abbey said. "Did they cut your budget?"

"Do you want your money?" Rollie said.

"You mean my grandfather's money," Abbey said. "And yes, he wants it."

"At his age, how long before you inherit it," Rollie said. "All you need do is wait him out."

"What do you want?" Abbey said. "Besides harassing me."

"I'm calling on behalf of the law firm of Gitter and Schram," Rollie said. "They have taken over the responsibility of the tontine. There is a great deal of paperwork to be filled out by your grandfather before the funds are released to him. They asked me to bring you to their office tomorrow at eleven o'clock to pick up the paperwork."

"Why can't they mail it?" Abbey said.

"I've seen the paperwork," Rollie said. "It's like a phone book of legalese. They need to explain certain things to you in person to make sure you not only grasp it but can explain it to your grandfather."

"Eleven o'clock where?" Abbey said.

"Got a pen handy?" Rollie said.

•   •   •

Rollie sat next to Grace as she drove his car to the mall in Valley Stream on Long Island. Giselle and Gloria occupied the back.

"Are we there yet," Gloria said.

"Don't start," Grace said.

"I still don't see why I need to go shopping," Rollie said. "I'll just give you the money and stay home."

"When was the last time you bought a new shirt?" Grace said. "Or a pair of slacks or shoes."

"It's been a while, Dad," Giselle said.

"I think I was still in diapers," Gloria said.

"Not that long," Rollie said.

"Long enough," Grace said.

"Are we there yet?" Rollie said.

Grace glared at Rollie and then she laughed, as did Giselle and Gloria.

•   •   •

"You can come in with us or you can wait here," Grace said.

"Why would I want to go in there?" Rollie said.

"Come on, girls," Grace said.

Holding a container of coffee, Rollie found a seat on a bench outside a woman's clothing store.

He was surrounded by crazed Christmas shoppers. Nauseating

holiday music played from speakers located throughout the mall.

Resigned to a long wait, Rollie took out his cell phone and called Joanna.

"Guess where I am?" Rollie said.

"The answer better not be with another woman," Joanna said.

"Three in fact," Rollie said.

"I hear Christmas music and a lot of noise," Joanna said. "I'm going to say the girls dragged you to a mall."

"They claim my clothes are very old fashioned and they are going to pick out what I should wear in South Carolina," Rollie said.

"Goodness," Joanna said.

"I'm not that out of date, am I?" Rollie said.

"Not to me, but I'm looking through forty-nine-year-old eyes," Joanna said.

"Maybe I could use a new belt or some socks," Rollie said.

"Relax. The girls are sensible," Joanna said.

They chatted for a few minutes and then Rollie said he would call later and put his phone away.

His coffee container empty, Rollie walked to the food court for another and then returned to the bench. Before he sat down, he looked at the store the girls were in and he saw Gloria at a spin rack with her back against the wall. A tall teenage boy had her trapped and was talking to her. The expression on her face told Rollie she was uncomfortable.

"Let's put a stop to this right now," Rollie said and started walking toward the store.

He was twenty feet from the store when Grace and Giselle suddenly appeared in front of the boy with fingers wagging. They chewed him out and sent him on his way.

"Big sisters to the rescue," Rollie said and returned to his seat on the bench.

A good hour passed and finally the girls came out of the store, each with three shopping bags.

"Your turn, Dad," Grace said.

"I hope you don't think I'm going in there," Rollie said.

"No, silly," Grace said.

"Macy's," Giselle said.

"The old man department," Gloria said.

"Gloria," Grace said.

"What? That's what you called it," Gloria said.

"It's after one," Rollie said. "Why don't we hit the food court and grab some lunch?"

.   .   .

Several hours later, Rollie and the girls walked to the car. Rollie had purchased three pairs of slacks, three shirts, three pullover shirts and a new pair of walking shoes.

"That wasn't so bad, was it?" Grace said.

They loaded everything into the trunk and Rollie tossed Grace the keys.

"You want me to drive?" Grace said.

"I just thought you might think I'm too old and might need a nap," Rollie said.

"Dad," Grace said.

"Home, James, and don't spare the gas," Rollie said.

"Who is James," Gloria said.

"It's a line from an old… never mind," Rollie said.

.   .   .

After thirty minutes on the step-climber and another thirty on the

Bowflex, Rollie toweled dry and called Teal at home.

"Are you free for lunch around one or so tomorrow?" Rollie said.

"Let me check my social calendar," Teal said. "Of course, I'm free. Why?"

"I'll tell you tomorrow," Rollie said.

"Anybody ever tell you that you're a real pain in the ass?" Teal said.

"Night, Bill," Rollie said.

CHAPTER FIFTY

Rollie parked his car in the garage a block from Gitter and Schram's office and was in their office by 9:30, giving him ample time to explain his plan.

Sipping coffee, Gitter said, "It sounds like a rather good way to get us both killed."

"You two are the golden goose, and you don't kill the golden goose," Rollie said. "Just let me carry the ball and don't let her intimidate you. She's got quite a nasty temper and mouth."

"Did anybody ever tell you you're a pain in the ass?" Schram said.

"No, nobody," Rollie said.

.   •   •

Wearing an expensive coat, Abbey arrived by cab a few minutes before eleven. Waiting for her in the lobby of the office building, Rollie stepped out to greet her.

Abbey greeted Rollie with, "Let's get this over with."

Neither spoke on the way up to Gitter and Schram's office.

In the conference room, Rollie made the introductions. "Abbigail Enache, Mr. Gitter, Mr. Schram, They have taken over the tontine in Rose's absence."

Abbey looked at the one-inch-thick folder on the table. "Is that it?" she said.

"If you mean the paperwork, yes, that is it," Gitter said,

"Well, let's get on with it then," Abbey said.

For forty-five minutes, Gitter and Schram read key paragraphs from the tontine bylaws and highlighted where Enache needed to sign.

"Is there anything you don't understand?" Gitter said.

"I'm not stupid," Abbey said. "I'll bring these home, have my grandfather sign and return them to you."

"There is one thing you should know before you leave," Gitter said. "As the legal representatives for the tontine, we have discretionary authority as to when to release the funds in the event we feel there is any wrongdoing involved."

"In short, we can hold onto the funds for years until we are satisfied a crime hasn't been committed," Schram said.

"Say, until after your grandfather passes away, and then all the money goes to charity," Gitter said. "And not one penny for you."

Abbey's eyes grew dark and cold. Her nostrils flared and her mouth formed a tight, thin line.

For a moment, she was motionless. Then she jumped to her feet and turned to Rollie.

"You fucking Irish prick, you put them up to this," Abbey said.

"That clause is in the bylaws for a reason," Gitter said.

"Oh, fuck you," Abbey said. "You haven't heard the last of this. I'll get a lawyer. I'll sue you. I'll take you to court."

"You mean your grandfather will," Rollie said.

Abbey glared at Rollie with a look of pure hatred and rage. Then her face softened and she smiled at Rollie. "We'll see each other again," she said.

"Don't forget your folder," Rollie said.

After Abbey left the conference room, Gitter sighed and said,

"Well, that went well."

.   .   .

"Sounds like she has quite the temper," Teal said as he bit into a chicken sandwich,

"I could see how she could drown Rose in the tub," Rollie said.

"Think that will work, delaying the money until after the old man is dead?" Teal asked.

"Legally it will work," Rollie said. "Gitter and Schram are certain of that."

"She's not going to go quietly into the good night," Teal said.

"No," Rollie said.

"She's killed eight, she could be thinking of making it nine?" Teal said.

"That is a possibility," Rollie said.

"You know what I think?" Teal said. "I think you painted a target on your back."

"She's smart, Bill," Rollie said. "She knows killing me doesn't get her the money. Just the opposite. It casts even more suspicion on her."

"Can she go after Gitter and Schram?" Teal said.

"That won't get her anything," Rollie said.

"Maybe not, but I don't trust her as far as I can spit," Teal said.

"We'll just have to wait and see what her next move is," Rollie said.

"And while we're waiting, don't drown in the bathtub," Teal said.

CHAPTER FIFTY-ONE

While the girls were at school, Rollie worked out on the step-climber and Bowflex machine, followed by a hot shower. He tossed on a comfortable warm-up suit and took a mug of coffee to his office.

He was scribbling notes to himself when the hard-line phone rang. He scooped it up and said, Rollie Finch."

Someone using a voice scrambler said, "You are in great danger," and hung up.

Rollie hit the redial button, but the number was scrambled as well.

He hung up and the phone rang again.

Again, someone using a voice scrambler said, "Your children are in great danger."

"Who is this?" Rollie said.

"Do I have your attention now?" the voice said.

"You got it. What do you want?" Rollie said.

Here's what's going to happen," the voice said. "You are going to convince those fucking lawyers to release the funds. If they refuse, one of your daughters dies a slow and painful death. You have until tomorrow to convince the lawyers."

"You're bluffing," Rollie said. "I know who this is. As soon as I hang up, I'm calling the police."

"Go ahead, but little Gloria will never be heard from again," the voice said.

Rollie was momentarily stunned.

"She's a cute kid," the voice said. "But if she lives to become a woman is entirely up to you."

"If you hurt my daughter," Rollie said.

"Blah fucking blah," the voice said.

"Listen, you psychotic bitch, I will kill you with my bare hands if my daughter is harmed," Rollie said.

"Whatever," the voice said. "You want your daughter, the price is $12,000,000, and remember this, you have two more."

"What do you want me to do?" Rollie said.

"Get those lawyers to release the funds," the voice said.

"Call back in five minutes," Rollie said and hung up.

Rollie used his cell phone to call Gloria's school. He told the administrator it was a family emergency and could they find Gloria right away. He held for five minutes until Gloria came on the line.

"Dad, what is it?" Gloria said.

"Nothing, go back to class," Rollie said.

He hung up and waited for the hard-line phone to ring.

It rang and he picked up the phone.

"By now you checked with her school and you know it was a bluff," the voice said. "The next one won't be. Have the lawyers sign the papers and I'll be around tonight to pick them up."

"What time?" Rollie said.

"Ten o'clock," the voice said. "And that fancy office building will be watched, so you'll be seen entering and leaving. Bring a copy of the signed paperwork to your home office and wait. At ten o'clock, someone will pick them up. And remember the helpless feeling you just had when you thought your daughter was missing. Don't make us do it for real."

The phone went dead in Rollie's hand.

He immediately called Teal.

"Bill, she made her move," Rollie said.

"What did she…?'

"Just listen," Rollie said. "Pick up my girls at the Ice Cream Dugout on Queens Boulevard and stash them someplace safe."

"Because?"

"She threatened to kill them if the papers aren't signed by Gitter and Schram," Rollie said.

"I'll send a car to pick her up," Teal said.

"She used one of those voice changers to disguise her voice," Rollie said. "And she used one of those number scramblers, so the call can't be traced. You pick her up and a lawyer will have her out in an hour."

"I'll take care of the girls," Teal said. "What are you going to do?"

"Wait," Rollie said.

"After I stash the girls, I'm waiting with you," Teal said.

"Ditch your car and come in the back door around six o'clock," Rollie said.

"I'll be there."

"My girls, Bill," Rollie said.

"With my life," Teal said.

"Call me when you have them."

Rollie hung up, changed quickly and drove his car to Manhattan. He took Queens Boulevard to the 59th Street Bridge into Manhattan. At five minutes past three, he called Grace's cell phone.

"Hi, Dad. I'm going to pick up—" Grace said.

"Grace, do as I say right now," Rollie said. "Drive your sisters to the Ice Cream Dugout and wait for your Uncle Bill to meet you at three thirty."

"Why, Dad? What's—"

"No questions, just do it, and don't get out of your car until you see Bill," Rollie said.

"Alright, Dad," Grace said.

Rollie hung up and drove like a trained cop, bobbing and weaving through traffic and parked in the lot a block from Gitter and Schram's office. As he walked to their office building, Teal called on the cell phone.

"Girls are with me," Teal said.

"Are they okay?"

"They're eating ice cream," Teal said.

"Thanks, Bill. I'll see you at six," Rollie said.

Rollie didn't kook around for a tail. Whoever was out there would be hidden or not at all and it was another bluff. Either way it didn't matter.

Gitter and Schram signed a copy of the documents giving Enache the funds. "Rollie, be careful," Schram said. "That girl is dangerous."

"That's why I asked you to sign," Rollie said.

"What now?" Gitter said.

"I go home and wait," Rollie said.

CHAPTER FIFTY-TWO

Shortly after six o'clock, Rollie and Teal drank coffee at Rollie's kitchen table. Except for a light on in the kitchen, the rest of the house was dark.

"I'd love nothing more than to arrest her on murder and kidnapping charges," Teal said.

"Evidence first," Rollie said. "Or she walks."

"You have the signed documents," Teal said.

"Made out to her grandfather and I can't identify the voice," Rollie said. "You pick her up now and a good defense lawyer gets her off and when Enache dies, she inherits it all, which was her plan to begin with."

"No way she gets away with eight murders," Teal said. "No fucking way."

Rollie got up to refill the coffee mugs and then claimed his chair at the table. "I think going back a year, Rose worked it out with her to take care of the competition like we figured," he said. "What they didn't figure on was an actual seventh man and after she killed him, Rose began to think she would make him number eight."

"Which she did," Teal said.

"Rose was probably in for $2,000,000, so with him gone she gets it all," Rollie said.

"She's not going to stop, you know that, right?" Teal said.

"She's the kind who leaves no evidence or witnesses behind, plus she likes killing. She's like that dog who tastes blood and then can't stop."

"What did Elizabeth say when you showed up with the girls and two detectives?" Rollie said.

"She asked the girls what they wanted for dinner," Teal said.

"Elizabeth is one in a million," Rollie said.

"She's been married to a cop for twenty-five years," Teal said. "She knows when not to ask questions."

"Did I tell you the girls and I are spending Christmas with Joanna?" Rollie said.

"No, you didn't," Teal said. "That's good. It's about time you got involved with a nice woman."

"The girls really like her and they get along great," Rollie said.

The hard-line phone rang on the wall rang and Rollie stood to answer the call. "Rollie Finch," he said.

"Hello, Mr. Finch. It's me, James Seymour. I need to ask Grace a question about today's homework assignment," James said.

"Are you at home?" Rollie said.

"Home, sir?"

"The place where you live," Rollie said.

"I'm doing my homework," James said.

"Never mind, I'll have her call you," Rollie said and hung up.

"Problem?" Teal said.

"The kid needs help with his homework," Rollie said. "Can you call Liz?"

Teal used his cell phone to call Elizabeth. "Hi, hon, it's me," he said. "Can I... everything is fine. Rollie needs to speak with Grace."

Teal handed Rollie the phone.

"Dad, what's going on?" Grace said. "Uncle Bill wouldn't tell us and..."

"Don't worry about it now," Rollie said. "James called and he needs help with your homework."

"Okay, I'll give him a call," Grace said.

"Put Liz back on the phone," Rollie said.

"Rollie?" Elizabeth said.

"Thanks, Liz," Rollie said. "I owe you one."

"Don't be ridiculous," Elizabeth said. "Put my fat husband on the phone."

Rollie handed Teal the phone.

"Your detectives brought their own donuts," Elizabeth said. "What kind of police department are you running, Bill?"

"I owe you one, too, hon," Teal said.

"From you, I'll collect," Elizabeth said. "Call me when whatever you scamps are up to is over," Elizabeth said.

Teal set the phone on the table. "I married the right woman," he said.

"I have a frozen pizza; want me to heat it up?" Rollie said.

.   •   •

"That's four slices for me," Teal said. "I'm stuffed."

"I'm going to let Buddy out in the backyard," Rollie said.

"Some fresh air would be nice," Teal said.

They went to Gloria's room and Teal patted the kittens for a few seconds. "They're getting big," he said.

"Buddy, let's get some air," Rollie said.

Buddy jumped down from the bed where he had been sleeping with the cat and followed Rollie and Teal to the kitchen.

"Company," Teal said.

Mama Cat had followed them and when Rollie opened the sliding doors, she entered the backyard with Buddy.

"Does she think she's a dog, or does Buddy think he's a cat?" Teal said.

"Mine is not to reason why," Rollie said.

"Ah, Shakespeare," Teal said.

Mama Cat sat beside the door and watched as Buddy sniffed his way around the yard.

Rollie gave them fifteen minutes before calling them inside.

"I'll make a fresh pot of coffee," Rollie said.

"Is it too late to send out for some donuts?" Teal said.

CHAPTER FIFTY-THREE

"How can you just sit there in the dark?" Teal said into Rollie's earpiece.

"I have the desk lamp on," Rollie said.

"You know what I mean," Teal said.

"You're the one in the dark," Rollie said.

Every light in the house was off and Teal waited just beyond the door that connected the house to the garage.

Rollie sipped coffee from a mug and looked out the open garage door at the dark street.

"Ever think we should have been firemen?" Teal said.

"I think they're called firefighters these days," Rollie said.

"And if my uncle was a woman, he'd be my aunt," Teal said.

"What does that even mean?" Rollie said.

"Hey, this is your house," Teal said.

"Quiet. She's here," Rollie said.

A shadow appeared in front of the open, garage door. Rollie switched on the tape recorder beside the lamp.

The shadow moved until it became a person.

Rollie watched as the person entered the garage. Dressed entirely in black, including ski mask and gloves, the person held a Glock 26 pistol in the right hand.

The person walked to a few feet in front of the desk.

Using a voice scrambler, the person said, "Am I going to need this?"

"No," Rollie said.

The person lowered the Glock.

"I expect that for the safety of your children, I have heard the last from you. Yes?" the person said.

"Yes," Rollie said.

"Fatherhood is a good thing," the person said. "It keeps you focused."

"Yes, it does," Rollie said.

"Are those the signed documents?" the person said.

"Yes," Rollie said. "Help yourself."

The person reached for the folder on the edge of the desk, and as the person leaned forward, Rollie brought up the .357 magnum revolver he had on his lap. The massive handgun appeared even larger because of the four-inch suppressor attached to the muzzle.

"What?" the person said as Rollie shot the person in the left shoulder.

On impact, the person was blown to the floor and Rollie was up and around the desk in an instant.

Teal, gun drawn, rushed into the garage.

Rollie knelt beside the person and took the Glock and tossed it to Teal. Then Rollie removed the ski mask to reveal the face of Bo Redford.

"Are you fucking shitting me," Teal said.

A strip of black, magnetic tape was on Redford's throat and Rollie removed it to disengage the voice scrambler.

"You shot me," Redford said.

"Why, Bo?" Rollie said.

Redford sighed.

"You can do twenty-five to life, or you can do twelve and a half to twenty-five," Teal said. "It all depends on how you answer the questions."

"I'm bleeding here," Redford said.

"And you'll continue to bleed unless you cooperate," Teal said.

"Maybe the third day, Abbey comes in my room and said, how would I like to have sex with her," Redford said. "You know me, Rollie, ladies man. Turns out she's the greatest piece of ass I've ever had. Pure gold. She says it can be permanent and I can split the money with her if."

Rollie sat on the edge of his desk. "You killed Funar and Rose?" he said.

"Yes. She killed all the others," Redford said. "What do I get for my testimony?"

"Talk that out with the DA," Teal said.

"I wouldn't have hurt your kids, Rollie," Redford said. "I couldn't help myself. It's always the crazy women who are great in bed, isn't it?"

"Bill, call an ambulance," Rollie said.

"Right, and then I'll have my guys arrest Abigail Enache for six counts of murder," Teal said.

CHAPTER FIFTY-FOUR

As Rollie and the girls walked through the gate at the airport, he spotted Joanna waiting for them. At the last minute, Rollie had booked a flight rather than drive.

The girls spotted Joanna and her face lit up like a Christmas tree. The girls raced through the gate and hugged Joanna.

Rollie came through the gate and Joanna stepped forward and hugged him. He leaned in close to her ear to whisper.

"It's not always the crazy women," Rollie said.

ABOUT THE AUTHOR

Al Lamanda was born and raised in New York City. For his work, he has been nominated for the Edgar Award, the Shamus Award, and won the Nero Wolfe Award for Best Mystery of the Year for his novel, *With 6 You Get Wally*, book five in the John Bekker Mysteries. The series continues with *Who Killed Joe Italiano?* (2018), *For Deader or Worse* (2019), and *The Case of the Missing Fan Dancer*, published by Encircle Publications in March, 2022.

In addition to his many mysteries, Al also writes Western novels under the name Ethan J. Wolfe, which have been highly received by the Western Historical Society. He served in the United States Marine Corps, and worked as a private investigator and professional bodyguard in New York, Massachusetts, and Florida. He also served as a security and loss prevention consultant for many large

ROLLIE AND THE MISSING SIX

corporations. In his free time, Al studied boxing, mixing it up in many amateur fights, and still trains today.

His latest stand-alone, the historical fiction novel, *City of Darkness*, was published by Encircle in January, 2021. He has published two Rollie Finch Mysteries, *Once Upon a Time on 9/11* (April, 2021), and *Rollie and the Missing Six* (August, 2022). Al is always working on his next novel.

If you enjoyed reading this book,
please consider writing your honest review
and sharing it with other readers.

Many of our Authors are happy to participate in
Book Club and Reader Group discussions.
For more information, contact us at info@encirclepub.com.

Thank you,
Encircle Publications

For news about more exciting new fiction, join us at:

Facebook: www.facebook.com/encirclepub

Instagram: www.instagram.com/encirclepublications

Twitter: twitter.com/encirclepub

Sign up for Encircle Publications newsletter and specials:
eepurl.com/cs8taP